MURDER
IN THE
MAP ROOM

Also by Elliott Roosevelt

Murder at Midnight
Murder in the Château
Murder in the Executive Mansion
A Royal Murder
Murder in the East Room
New Deal for Death
Murder in the West Wing
Murder in the Red Room
The President's Man
A First-Class Murder
Murder in the Blue Room
Murder in the Rose Garden
Murder in the Oval Office
Murder at the Palace
The White House Pantry Murder
Murder at Hobcaw Barony
The Hyde Park Murder
Murder and the First Lady

Perfect Crimes (ed.)

MURDER
IN THE
MAP ROOM

An Eleanor Roosevelt Mystery

Elliott Roosevelt

St. Martin's Press
New York

Doubleday Direct Large Print Edition

This Large Print Edition, prepared especially for Doubleday Direct, Inc., contains the complete unabridged text of the original Publisher's Edition.

Production Editor: David Stanford Burr

ISBN 1-56865-797-8

PRINTED IN THE UNITED STATES

This Large Print Book carries the Seal of Approval of N.A.V.H.

I

On January 31, 1943, German Field Marshal Friedrich Paulus surrendered at Stalingrad.

Ten days later the last surviving Japanese troops abandoned Guadalcanal.

Two weeks later Field Marshal Erwin Rommel defeated an American force at the Kasserine Pass in Tunisia. It was the last German victory in North Africa. A week after Kasserine, American forces drove Rommel back and exhausted his dwindling army. He reported to Hitler that North Africa was lost and asked for permission to evacuate what was left of the Afrika Korps.

Though few realized it, the tide of the war had decisively shifted. Hard and costly fighting remained, but after February 1943, the Axis powers were in retreat. How the war would end was no longer in question.

* * *

On the same day when Paulus surrendered at Stalingrad, President Franklin D. Roosevelt returned to Washington after a mysterious absence of more than two weeks. Only after he was back in the White House was it announced that he had been to Casablanca, where he had conferred at length with Prime Minister Winston Churchill, General Charles de Gaulle, and with Allied military leaders, including Generals Dwight Eisenhower and George Patton.

His visit to Casablanca also had a personal significance for him, and for Mrs. Roosevelt, since in Casablanca he had been able to spend a little time with two of his sons. The destroyer on which Franklin junior was serving happened to be at Casablanca. Elliott's air unit was stationed in North Africa. The President came home with a cheerful report of how the boys looked, what they said, and what they were doing. Mrs. Roosevelt was pleased. Her sons, she sometimes complained, were not the best of letter writers.

She was not as well pleased with the President's health. He was obviously exhausted. Churchill had insisted they drive

I

On January 31, 1943, German Field Marshal Friedrich Paulus surrendered at Stalingrad.

Ten days later the last surviving Japanese troops abandoned Guadalcanal.

Two weeks later Field Marshal Erwin Rommel defeated an American force at the Kasserine Pass in Tunisia. It was the last German victory in North Africa. A week after Kasserine, American forces drove Rommel back and exhausted his dwindling army. He reported to Hitler that North Africa was lost and asked for permission to evacuate what was left of the Afrika Korps.

Though few realized it, the tide of the war had decisively shifted. Hard and costly fighting remained, but after February 1943, the Axis powers were in retreat. How the war would end was no longer in question.

* * *

On the same day when Paulus surrendered at Stalingrad, President Franklin D. Roosevelt returned to Washington after a mysterious absence of more than two weeks. Only after he was back in the White House was it announced that he had been to Casablanca, where he had conferred at length with Prime Minister Winston Churchill, General Charles de Gaulle, and with Allied military leaders, including Generals Dwight Eisenhower and George Patton.

His visit to Casablanca also had a personal significance for him, and for Mrs. Roosevelt, since in Casablanca he had been able to spend a little time with two of his sons. The destroyer on which Franklin junior was serving happened to be at Casablanca. Elliott's air unit was stationed in North Africa. The President came home with a cheerful report of how the boys looked, what they said, and what they were doing. Mrs. Roosevelt was pleased. Her sons, she sometimes complained, were not the best of letter writers.

She was not as well pleased with the President's health. He was obviously exhausted. Churchill had insisted they drive

150 miles across the desert to Marrakech, which he regarded as a romantic town, famous for its fortune-tellers, snake charmers, and brothels—plus one of the world's most beautiful views: the sight of the sun setting over the Atlas Mountains. The President had endured this drive and had allowed himself to be carried to the roof of a villa, to view the sunset Churchill had brought him all this way to see. The next day he had flown to the British colony of Gambia, where he had insisted on taking a cruise up the Gambia River. Later he would tell Churchill he had contracted "Gambia fever." He flew on to Liberia for a luncheon with its president. From there he flew to Brazil and conferred with *its* president.

The President did not enjoy flying. He enjoyed travel by ship and by train, but he complained that staring at the clouds was boring. "Anyway, it affects my head," he told Mrs. Roosevelt—by which he meant it caused sinus pain. He had managed to rest on the train ride to Washington, but when she saw him she saw a man tired and fevered and in need of rest.

Which he could not have—not the

President of the United States in the second year of a major war.

She had been surprised—pleased and surprised—by the way he had so far carried the immense burdens of his office in wartime. He was sixty-one years old. The very simplest things in life—rising from a chair, sitting down again, taking a bath, going to bed, getting up—not to mention entering or leaving a car or boarding an airplane—were physical ordeals for him, no matter how much help he had. Still, he met the challenges of leadership and even seemed to thrive on them.

Seemed to thrive on them . . . She saw, as others less sensitive to him did not, that his burden was taking a toll.

The President had lost many of the people who had helped him. Louis Howe was of course long dead. Jim Farley had decided he didn't want to be a friend any longer. The children were scattered all over the world. Missy LeHand was gravely ill and no longer able to give him the companionship that had meant so much to him through thousands of evenings that would have otherwise been unbearably lonely. Harry Hopkins and his wife lived in the White House, but he *was* living with his new wife and was besides overworked and in failing health.

The First Lady had long since accepted her own shortcoming: that she simply was not capable of easy banter over cocktails and dinner, the kind of relaxing conversation the President needed and loved. She could never forget that some problem needed his attention, and she could never resist the urgent impulse to bring it to his attention. The unhappy fact was that she and the President could not relax together.

And they could not this evening, the evening of the thirty-first of January, when he lay in his bed, propped up on pillows, taking his dinner from the usual tray. She sat beside him but would not eat, since she was dining with friends downstairs a little later. He frowned skeptically over the unappetizing meal he found on his plate—another dinner of what he called "rubber chicken."

Mrs. Roosevelt continued a conversation they had already begun. "I think you may find," she said to the President, "that the visit by Madame Chiang will prove refreshing as well as useful."

"I'd as soon confront a black widow spider," he said. "If Winston's heaviest cross is the Cross of Lorraine, one of mine, if not *the* heaviest, is that shaven-headed egomaniac and his harridan wife."

"Franklin!"

"I wonder what, exactly is the relationship between her and Henry Luce. Why does he sell out to her and her husband so unconscionably?"

"Franklin . . ."

"I've seen *Time* and *Life*," he said. "Oh, our country is immeasurably blessed. Saint Mei-ling of Chungking has deigned to set foot on our soil."

"I visited her at the hospital in New York," said Mrs. Roosevelt. "She's a very dear woman, really. Kind and generous. She's at Hyde Park now. I offered her the use of the house until she is sufficiently recovered to come to Washington."

"Well . . . mother's dead. At least *she* doesn't have to tolerate the woman."

"Franklin . . . Madame Chiang Kai-shek will be addressing a joint session of Congress during her visit."

"Of course. All she'll ask for is that we abandon the war in Europe and concentrate all the armed forces of the United States and Britain on the war in the Pacific. Well, she can forget that. That's settled. Given a choice between being knifed by Chiang or bludgeoned by Stalin, Winston and I decided to be knifed. And so we will be. And he's sent the Dragon Lady to do it."

"Well, you have about two weeks to improve your disposition and develop a warmer attitude toward a woman I have come to know as a gentle, sweet character."

"I shall think of nothing else till the day she arrives," said the President.

That day was February 17.

Madame Chiang Kai-shek had been born Soong Mei-ling forty-six years ago. She was the daughter of a shrewd Chinese businessman who had amassed a fortune by selling Bibles. She was one of three sisters. Soong Ai-ling was married to H. H. Kung, seventy-fifth in direct lineal descent from K'ung-Fu-tzu, who was known in the

West as Confucius. H. H. Kung was China's minister of finance, though it was widely reported in the West that he understood nothing of money that was not made of copper, silver, or gold. Soong Ming-ling was the widow of Dr. Sun Yat-sen, nationalist leader and the most popular president the Chinese republic ever had.

Madame Chiang had been educated at Wellesley (class of 1917) and spoke fluent, unaccented English—coping with every nuance of American English from the most obscure diplomatic subtleties to the coarsest vulgarities. She was a Christian—a Methodist—and had convinced her husband to convert.

Madame Chiang was a political power in her own right. Her family connections had contributed immeasurably to her husband's rise. When the Generalissimo, as he styled himself, was kidnapped by rebels in 1936 and held prisoner for two weeks, Soong family prestige and Madame Chiang's determination and diplomatic skills were important factors in securing his release. She was the darling of the China Lobby in the U.S. Congress, and she enjoyed what amounted to adoration from Henry Luce, the publisher of *Time* and *Life*. No Chinese was better known and better liked by Americans than Madame Chiang Kai-shek.

The President had to keep her popularity in mind as he received her at the White House.

She had been injured in an automobile accident in China and had come to the United States for medical treatment and spent her first weeks in New York, where she and her staff occupied a whole floor of a prestigious hospital. Then she spent some time at Hyde Park. February 17 was a Wednesday. She would be a guest at the White House the rest of that week and all of the next, after which she would tour the States for several weeks.

Her chief of staff arrived on the fifteenth. His name was Weng Guo-fang, and he was a fragile little old man with a deeply wrinkled face, wispy white mustache and goatee, a hunched posture, and a dry cough. He wore beautifully tailored suits of soft wool. His speech was elaborately polite and deferential when he spoke to Mrs. Roosevelt but—though still polite—quite curt and firm when he spoke to anyone he supposed was a servant. It was quite plain that he divided people into classes and treated them accordingly. The First Lady found that difficult to tolerate— though she made a due allowance for his age and for the cultural difference.

He inspected the suite Madame Chiang was to occupy and asked for changes. He explained that Madame Chiang carried her own bedclothes—silk sheets and pillow cases. If she lay down on her bed even for a few minutes, her servants would strip the bed and remake it with fresh silk. All her sheets had to be ironed several times a day, to be sure she did not lie down on a wrinkle. She would not eat the ordinary White House diet. The housekeeper, Mrs. Nesbitt, was given detailed instructions about what Madame Chiang ate and how it must be prepared.

Weng Guo-fang was apologetically tactful; yet he made it plain that Madame expected these concessions.

"Just who the devil does she think she is?" the President asked irritably.

"Let me remind you of something, Franklin," said Mrs. Roosevelt. "When our son Jimmy was in China, he was suffering a great deal of pain from his ulcer, a problem that had been compounded by the food he had to eat as he traveled. Madame Chiang found out about this and saw to it that he was given a proper diet for an ulcer patient. She prepared many of his meals with her own hands. If she can do that for us, I guess we can tolerate her dietary requirements while she is our guest."

"Even so, I wish she were not coming," said the President. "Her dietary demands will be the least of her demands."

Mrs. Roosevelt was long accustomed to how her husband could change his colors, as dramatically as a chameleon and infinitely faster. Meeting Madame Chiang at Union Station, he treated her as if she were an old, old friend he had long yearned to see again. In fact, as soon as they were in the car together, he asked her with a sly smile what she thought of Wendell Willkie.

Wendell Willkie had been the President's opponent in the 1940 election. Subsequently he had toured the world, meeting the leaders of various nations and gathering the impressions that would become the subject of his book *One World*. Among those he had visited and apparently impressed with his personal magnetism was Generalissimo Chiang Kai-shek and Madame Chiang.

"Ah, Mr. Willkie is charming!" Madame Chiang replied to the President's question.

"Of course. But what do you *really* think of him?" the President persisted.

"Well," said the First Lady of China, after a brief hesitation, "he is, after all, still an adolescent."

The President laughed. "Oh, ho! So, then, what do you think of *me?*"

"Mr. President," she said instantly, *"You* are very sophisticated."

In that exchange, a new relationship was born. The President's hostility toward Madame Chiang, if it did not die, was significantly diminished. Hers toward him— arising from the fact that the Generalissimo had not been invited to the Casablanca Conference—slipped away into invisibility.

In any case, as the First Lady had anticipated, Soong Mei-ling, Madame Chiang Kai-shek, was the sort of woman the President instinctively liked.

She was, to begin with, diminutive.

That was part of her charm—and her charm was formidable. Her skin was pale and soft. Her makeup was understated but exquisitely contrived and flattering to suggest she was younger than her forty-six years. Her nails were rapier long. Mrs. Roosevelt wondered how a woman who carried the burdens this woman had to carry could manage to find time during each day to undergo the beauty care she obviously required. She was like a fine automobile or airplane that required constant maintenance. No doubt she was massaged each day from head to toe with creams and oils. Her hair must have required half an hour's attention every day. Her cosmetics . . .

Obviously she regarded all these things as essential.

She wore an ankle-length black silk dress, ornamented with chips of jade sewn here and there. The collar was fastened just beneath her chin and ears. Yet, the dress was not modest. It clung to her figure. Also, the skirt was slit on each side. When she sat the slits exposed her bare legs to the knee and sometimes even a little above.

It would have been foolish to use the term *modest* about this woman. That word meant nothing to her. She was steel-hard, aggressive, and ruthless. She was also crafty, subtle, and wary. She identified her advantages and used them. She had sometimes done so at the risk of her life.

She used the fact that she was an exceptionally handsome woman, just as she used the fact that she was a Christian (and a Methodist at that), to dazzle men far more perceptive than the senators and representatives she was going to meet on this trip, far more perceptive than the dull-witted Henry Luce.

She was the wife of a "generalissimo." No queen was ever more regal. As the First Lady was shortly to observe, when she entered a room, she dominated it. What was more, there was no question but that she meant to dominate.

"I am very much looking forward to Eleanor's visit to China," said Madame Chiang in the car.

The President glanced past her and for an instant caught the eye of the First Lady, who was able to convey that she had no idea what China's First Lady was talking about.

"Well, that's something we're looking into," said the President. He did not say that he had no intention whatever of allowing Mrs. Roosevelt to travel to China. "There are some arrangements to be made."

"Of course," said Madame Chiang, who entirely understood the implication of what he had said.

At the White House, confusion reigned. Which suite the famous guest would occupy was well understood: the elegant Queen's Suite that had been occupied by Queen Elizabeth on the occasion of the visit of King George VI and the Queen in 1939. The difficulty was with Madame Chiang's staff.

She had brought with her a nephew and a niece, invariably referred to as Mr. Kung and Miss Kung, as private secretaries. (They were the children of the seventy-fifth lineal descendant of Confucius and were never modest about informing people that they were the seventy-sixth lineal descendants.) The difficulty was that Miss Kung dressed as a man, always; and being slight, with her hair cut short, was taken by many Americans as a young man. Mrs. Roosevelt had assigned Miss Kung to a room and instructed the White House staff to take her there and unpack her things. Shortly, an usher came to the First Lady, flustered, saying a mistake had been made, that the person assigned to *that* room was a young man. While Mrs. Roosevelt was dealing with that embarrassed usher, another arrived, saying that the maid unpacking the young man's luggage had found that nearly everything in his bags—underclothes, nightclothes, cosmetics—were a woman's!

The guests for dinner that first night of Madame Chiang's visit were only the President and Mrs. Roosevelt, Madame Chiang, Weng Guo-fang—dressed for the evening in black silk cap, embroidered yellow silk jacket, and black silk trousers—Mr. Kung and Miss Kung, Harry Hopkins and his wife, Louise, and Congresswoman Helen Gahagan Douglas. They met first in the President's study, the oval room adjacent to the family suites.

The President, as always, took delight in the conviviality of the cocktail hour. This evening he took delight also in the company of the glamorous and sophisticated First Lady of China. Wearing another black silk dress, this one with even higher slits in the skirt, she stayed near the President throughout the hour and encouraged him to talk about the war and the strategy he believed would win it.

She said nothing of the resentment Mrs. Roosevelt knew she felt about the Casablanca Conference. She had spat that out in the hospital in New York, when she had told Mrs. Roosevelt there was no point in China staying in the war and fighting the Japanese if China were not to be regarded as an equal partner in a great, four-power coalition: the United States, Great Britain, Soviet Russia, *and China.* We are equal partners, she had said bitterly, or we are not partners at all. So, how dare the President and Churchill meet without the Generalissimo? That Stalin refused to meet Chiang was understood, since the Soviet Union was not at war with Japan; but the United States, Great Britain, and China were allies in a grand coalition, so how could Roosevelt and Churchill meet alone to discuss strategy? No decision they

could take could possibly be valid without
the concurrence of Generalissimo Chiang
Kai-shek.

Tonight, though, she showed nothing
of the tough Madame Chiang. She
charmed the President. Mrs. Roosevelt almost regretted she had given the First
Lady of China some instruction into winning the confidence and support of the
President of the United States.

One awkward moment. Madame
Chiang introduced her nephew and niece
to the President. He did not quite hear
what she said, and he smiled and nodded
to Miss Kung and said—

"Well, it's very nice to meet you, my
boy."

Harry Hopkins quickly scribbled a
note and slipped it to the President—in
time for the President to say to Miss Kung,
"You understand that I address all interesting young people as 'my boy.'"

It was weak, but it worked. Miss Kung
smiled and said she had heard that he did.

The truth, as Mrs. Roosevelt guessed,
was that Miss Kung was not in the least
offended. Dressing as a man, as report-
edly she invariably did, helped her to

overcome the male prejudices that still very much governed society and government in China. Weng Guo-fang's heavy-lidded eyes expressed his disapproval of Miss Kung; but no one else, once the matter was understood, either approved or disapproved.

Over dinner, Madame Chiang did gently raise with the President the question of the strategy agreed upon among the other three leaders—what was called the "Germany first" strategy.

"This country," she said to the President, in a voice so low she obviously meant to be heard by him alone and not by anyone else at that dinner, "entered the war, not because of anything Hitler did, but because of what Japan did at Pearl Harbor, followed by Japanese atrocities in the Philippines, Hong Kong, Singapore, and so on. Americans hate Japan. To let Japan continue to run wild in Asia while you concentrate your resources on defeating Hitler—"

"We have committed major forces to the Pacific Theater."

"Will you deny, Mr. President, that

your overall strategy for winning this war is to defeat Germany first?"

"I cannot confirm or deny it."

"Well, Mr. President, there are those who believe—I am not among them—that the United States is far more concerned about aggression against the British, the French, et cetera—the white races, in other words—than about aggression against Orientals."

"Hitler is the greater threat," said the President. "If he should defeat Russia and—"

"What if Japan defeats all our forces in Asia and becomes the ruler, not just of China, but of Burma and India? Which is the greater threat then? Australia and New Zealand fall, of course. And then what?"

"It's been considered," said the President.

Madame Chiang let the President see a cynical smile the First Lady had seen before and he had not. "All of this *must* be carefully considered, Mr. President," she said. "What concerns me is that when you meet with Churchill—or meet with Stalin, as you will—you will be meeting with the leaders of countries threatened only by

Hitler. They will convince you that *their* salvation is imperative. All I ask, Mr. President, is that you consider what results will befall if Japan attains its goals in Asia."

The President glanced at Mrs. Roosevelt—an "I told you so" glance.

"But let us not darken a lovely dinner with talk of global strategy," said Madame Chiang. "I will welcome the opportunity of talking with you about it again. For now—"

She raised her glass of wine. "Mr. President. Your health and success—and those of the American people."

Five minutes later, Mrs. Roosevelt had to lean close to the President and Madame Chiang to witness another element of her character.

"Do you enjoy little jokes, Mr. President?"

"I do, very much."

"Well . . . It seems there was this American Indian. A doctor advised him that he should have been circumcised as an infant and suggested the operation should be performed now. The Indian was skeptical, but he asked what the fee would be. "One hundred dollars," said the doctor. "Ugh, too much," said the Indian. So he went to another doctor and asked what his fee would be. The doctor said eighty dollars. "Ugh, too much," said the Indian. A third doctor asked only sixty dollars, but— "Ugh, too much." So . . . "Do him myself," said the Indian. He put his male organ on a stump, wielded his axe, and, looking down in horror, exclaimed— *"Ugh! Too much!"*

The President laughed, but Mrs. Roosevelt doubted he had enjoyed the joke. He had never appreciated that kind of humor. As for herself— Well . . . By reputation, she would have been offended. In truth, she shrugged and chuckled and promptly forgot the little story.

Weng Guo-fang's lips tightened, and he did not laugh. The First Lady took note that Madame Chiang's chief of staff was a man with sufficient stature to show his disapproval of her. She wondered who he really was.

The joke was not interesting. That Madame Chiang told it was decidedly interesting. She had a catholic armamentarium.

The First Lady watched the President closely, trying to judge to what degree he had changed his mind about this woman he had called "Dragon Lady." She had hoped he would find some sympathy for this magnificent woman and her besieged people. Now, though her sentiments toward China had not changed in the least, she was not sure she wanted to see Franklin influenced by—

By what? Whom? A woman who had broken free from male constraints and made herself a popular leader? A jezebel?

Her visit to the White House was going to be more interesting than anyone had imagined.

"I beg your pardon," said Mrs. Roosevelt. "I shall return in a moment."

Statecraft requires, almost above all else, unyielding control of the bladder. The statesman who must abandon the conference table from time to time to make a visit to the bathroom earns the contempt of his fellow statesmen. It is with them a matter of pride. Hold your water and negotiate. Hold it until the other fellow can't.

Of such things is international policy concocted.

The American First Lady ordinarily

played the game well. Tonight, for some reason, she was compelled to go.

The intimate dinner for Madame Chiang that first night of her visit was in the small private dining room, north of the State Dining Room. Leaving that room, a quick visit to her own suite on the second floor—where she could check her makeup and hair and even look at her telephone messages—was as convenient as any bathroom on the ceremonial first floor. She walked out through the east door of the private dining room and into the small private elevator the custodians of the White House called Elevator Number 1.

The usher who operated the elevator appeared oddly nervous but said nothing.

Leaving the elevator, she walked into the Center Hall. To her right was the West Sitting Hall, where the President usually sat in early evenings and enjoyed his cocktail hour. To the left and some ten yards to the east were the double doors that separated the private quarters of the White House from the second-floor public rooms.

The rooms were laid out like this—

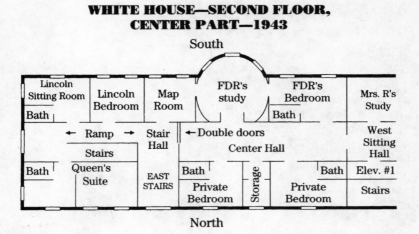

**WHITE HOUSE—SECOND FLOOR,
CENTER PART—1943**

A uniformed White House policeman stood guard at the double doors. That was unusual, and she walked over to ask why.

"Excuse me, Ma'am," he said. "Let me ask Mr. Kirkwal to speak to you."

He stepped away from the door for a moment and went into the Map Room just beyond. A Secret Service agent the First Lady recognized as Robert Kirkwal came out.

"What's going on, Mr. Kirkwal?"

"I'm sorry, Ma'am. There's been a murder here. Ugly sight, I'm afraid. In the Map Room."

II

Mrs. Roosevelt did not know Robert Kirkwal very well, though he had served in the White House for as long as she had been there. He had just been one of the Secret Service agents who was always around but with whom she had had minimal contact.

Poor Gerald Baines, who had been so shrewd and effective in investigation, was still in prison as the result of his role in the White House pantry murders last year. Dominic Deconcini was serving in the Marine Corps in the Pacific. Stanislas Scziegel had retired. This man, Kirkwal, was what was left.

No. That was unfair. Mr. Kirkwal might well be just as competent as any of the others. Perhaps he needed a chance to prove himself.

Certainly he was the most handsome of all the Secret Service men she had ever seen. His face was strong and square. He had a pronounced cleft in his chin. His eyes were dark and intense. His lower lip protruded a bit. His hair, which obviously had been black, was now iron gray; but it remained thick, and he kept it neatly combed with some sort of dressing with a faint pleasant odor. He spoke with a faint accent she could not quite identify. It sounded a little like the Cockney speech of east London. Maybe the most characteristic thing about him was that his face at rest settled into a faintly cynical smile, as if he were a skeptical observer and found amusement in everyone and everything.

"Mr. Kirkwal," she said firmly, sensing that he wanted her to retreat now that she had heard that murder had been committed in the White House—retreat and leave the problem to him. "Who has been murdered?"

"I don't know who the man is, Ma'am. An Oriental. Chinese, maybe. Or Japanese."

"I must see him," she said emphatically.

"Ma'am . . . His throat was cut. He—"

"Mr. Kirkwal, I have to see him. I have to know if he's one of the people Madame Chiang brought with her."

"A ghastly sight, Ma'am."

"I've seen them before, Mr. Kirkwal."

He stood aside and pointed toward the door of the Map Room.

The second-floor room that in 1943 served as Map Room had served over the decades in various ways and had been called by various names, lately the Monroe Room, though Cabinet Room during the administrations of Andrew Johnson and U. S. Grant. Mrs. Herbert Hoover had used it as a private study. Mrs. Roosevelt had held her press conferences there. When Winston Churchill visited the White House in December 1941, he had told the President he should have a map room, with every latest movement on all fronts carefully marked, every hour, every day. He had in fact assigned two of his staff to help the President's staff in setting up the Map Room, to be much like his own in London. There was a Situation Room on the ground floor, which the President could visit to review developments, but the Map Room was a convenient resource for him, adjacent to his study, and he went in several times a day to stare at the maps and visualize the state of the war.

The Map Room was supposed to be a secure room. Although no great military secrets were reflected on the maps—the enemy nations knew, after all, what territory they held and didn't hold—the room was attended every day by army and navy officers and kept locked when those officers were not present.

The first question that troubled the First Lady as she entered the room was how the dead man had gotten in.

He lay in the center of the room. His body was drawn up into a sort of fetal position and lay on its side. He was, she saw immediately, a well-dressed, compact Oriental man. He might have been asleep except that his throat had been cut and his blood had stained his white shirt, his blue necktie, and his dark-blue suit—also the carpet.

Mrs. Roosevelt stared at his face. She did not recognize him as a member of Madame Chiang's staff—and that, anyway, was a relief.

"Mr. Kirkwal," she said. "I am sure you realize the delicacy of the situation."

"I do, indeed, Ma'am."

"Telephone Captain Edward Kennelly, Chief of Detectives, District of Columbia police. Speak to no one else. Call his home number if you must. Use my name to get that number if they won't otherwise give it to you. Tell Captain Kennelly that we need him here, on a most confidential matter. Tell him I said you should contact him. You may trust Captain Kennelly to be circumspect."

Kirkwal nodded. "Captain Edward Kennelly," he repeated.

"It is essential, if we can possibly manage it, that Madame Chiang and her people not learn that murder has been committed in the White House tonight, within a few yards of the entrance to their bedrooms—not to mention within a few yards of the President's. I don't think this man is a member of Madame Chiang's group, but we must learn who he is as quickly as possible."

Robert Kirkwal frowned thoughtfully. She understood that he was uncertain as to how much authority the First Lady had over a criminal investigation, whether in the White House or otherwise. Then she saw his frown fade. He had decided, apparently, that it would be unwise to challenge her.

"I must return to the dinner for Madame Chiang. But I will come back here as soon as I can break away. Please keep the door closed. The body must not be removed until we are certain the Chinese have all gone to bed. I should not want them to step out into the hall and see a corpse being carried out."

"The Soviet Union is not at war with Japan," the President said to Madame Chiang. "His refusal to meet with the Generalissimo is nothing personal. It does not, I am sure, mean any want of respect. But we have to remember, that Hitler's armies are far inside Russia, and the Russians are fighting for their lives. A Japanese invasion on the Pacific coast of the Soviet Union would be more than Stalin could cope with. He'd have to let the Japanese run rampant through the Asiatic provinces of the Soviet Union because he hasn't a soldier to spare."

The President lifted his wineglass and sipped approvingly and appreciatively. Because Madame Chiang's advance staff had made it clear that Madame would be offended by the cheap and unpalatable wines that usually came up, in thimbleful amounts, from the White House pantry, a supply of good French Bordeaux had been put in for her visit.

"What do you suppose would happen," he went on, "if Hitler defeated Stalin? German and Japanese armies would meet in, say, India. And where would China be then? Where would we be? Where would the British be?"

"Our alliance is an alliance of *four* powers," said Madame Chiang.

"Granted."

"And therefore, no two or three can make decisions on global strategy without the concurrence of the fourth."

"I assume," said the President smoothly, "that such is the purpose of your visit. You are here as the representative of the Generalissimo, to hear from me personally a full report of the discussions

I had with the Prime Minister two weeks ago. I have no doubt you have points of view to present. I can't tell you how pleased I am to have this marvelous opportunity to exchange views."

Even for the woman who had been married to him for thirty-eight years, this was a little too much; and the First Lady caught her husband's eye with a disapproving glance. What she wanted to say was: If you think you can out-charm this woman, be careful; she plays that game in the same league you do.

"I, too, am very pleased, Mr. President. Have you any suggestions as to what I should say in my address to the Congress?"

Mrs. Roosevelt smiled to herself. Slash, riposte, slash. The President might be meeting his match.

Even as Madame Chiang fell silent and listened in apparently rapt attention to a presidential monologue on military logistics, she was still slashing away in their duel of wits—because she had obviously observed, or maybe had been told, that Franklin D. Roosevelt favored women who were good listeners.

* * *

Almost a full hour passed before the dinner ended and Mrs. Roosevelt could return to the Map Room. She accompanied Madame Chiang to the door of her suite, then hurried past the closed door of the Map Room and to the President's suite, to say good-night to him. She chose not to tell him about the murder. Maybe by the time she had to tell him, in the morning, she would be able to say who the dead man was, maybe even who had killed him.

She knocked on the door of the Map Room. It was opened by Agent Kirkwal. She walked in, to find Captain Edward Kennelly was there, as was a young man who sat uneasily and seemed to be waiting for something and maybe dreading it. The body still lay on the floor, covered with a sheet.

"Captain Kennelly," she said. "It is good to see you again—even if the circumstances are distressing."

Kennelly was a tall, red-faced, white-haired Irishman. She had met him as long ago as 1934, when he took part in the investigation of the murder of Congressman

Winstead Coleman, who had been shot to death in the Oval Office itself; and she had worked with him several times since. As he rose to greet her, he crushed out a Lucky.

"Mrs. Roosevelt," he said. " 'Tis an honor as always." He spoke with an Irish brogue and had often amused the First Lady with peculiarities of speech—such as consistently referring to Sir Alan Burton as "Sir Burton." He was a careful and professional investigator, even so. She respected him as much as he respected her. "We've got another little problem on our hands."

"So I see."

Kennelly nodded toward the young man sitting apprehensively and a little apart. "This is Dr. William Gray," he said. "He is the medical examiner. He's a good man, I can assure you—though it took nothing much to establish how this man died."

Mrs. Roosevelt stepped over toward the doctor, who rose instantly. "I am pleased to meet you, Dr. Gray," she said. "I am sure Captain Kennelly has explained the necessity of your keeping this matter absolutely confidential."

The young doctor nodded.

"I told him," said Kennelly, "that his career as a doctor would be over once and for all if he breathed a word outside this room."

Mrs. Roosevelt smiled at the doctor, meaning to reassure him a little and seeing that her smile didn't reassure him at all. Well— Maybe it was just as well he remain a little overimpressed.

"Captain Kennelly, I assume you and Mr. Kirkwal have established a working relationship," she said.

She meant she hoped they had clarified any problem of jurisdiction. That could have been thorny, but Kennelly had always cooperated and received cooperation. The point was that the Secret Service was technically responsible for the protection of the President, his family, and certain other officials. It was not an investigative agency. Its men were not detectives. The same was true of the uniformed White House police, who were responsible for guarding the premises. A crime committed in the White House or on the grounds came within the jurisdiction of the District of Columbia police—although from time to time J. Edgar Hoover claimed that such crimes fell within the jurisdiction of the FBI. Besides all that, the Army was also guarding the White House in wartime, and its officers might have to be consulted about how the murderer and victim got in.

"We will have no problems," Kirkwal promised.

"So, then. Have you identified the victim?"

"He is an American of Chinese ancestry," said Kirkwal. "His name is George Shen. He was carrying documents that pretty firmly establish that."

"May I know what those documents are?"

"You may examine them," said Kennelly. "Here's his California driver's license."

The First Lady examined the limp document—limp because it had been carried in a wallet for months. The carrier of the license was identified as Shen, George C., 412 Sacramento Street, San Francisco, California, 41 years old, 5' 8", 154 pounds, eyes dark, hair dark, race Chinese.

"Anyone could be carrying this," she said.

"Anyone that height, weight, age, and ancestry," said Kirkwal.

"Persuasive evidence of identification—but not conclusive," she said.

Kennelly grinned at Kirkwal. "What'd I tell ya? Mrs. Roosevelt knows her business."

Robert Kirkwal—as the First Lady was going to see time and again—was a man of odd charm that defined description. Just now, for example, he shrugged and smiled and raised both his eyebrows. "I'd no suspicion it would be otherwise," he said.

"There are other papers you oughta see," said Kennelly. "Like this here—"

He handed her a crumpled sheet of writing paper that had been smoothed out. It was a personal, handwritten letter.

Dear George,
Glad to hear from you. They got no right to make you travel as far as Wash. and I am not happy with that. They got no right to send you so far away when we are just a little time from the happy day. What with the way train travel is these days, <u>you might not</u>

<u>make it back on time!</u> Promise me, no fooling, you will get away from there in plenty of time. I can't think of anything worse than getting a wire saying you're stuck in St. Louis or someplace and— Well, you know. It <u>can't</u> happen, honey! Don't play around.

What's worse, I hear that Madam Peanut is coming to Wash. I hope the Prez sees through her—that oughta take him about five minutes. Don't let nobody give you some kind of idea that you oughta stay in town and pay her some kind of honor. The only honor you owe anybody is to <u>me,</u> meaning you get back here in time for the parties and all the rest of it. I mean, for sure!

You know how much love all of us send you. Maybe you don't really know how much I send from <u>me.</u> No fooling around, honey man. Nothing's more important.

The most love and kisses ever,
Yu-lin

Tears came to Mrs. Roosevelt's eyes as she read the letter. The bloody corpse lying under that sheet had been a young woman's bridegroom for a wedding not many days away.

"The word—"

"Has gone to San Francisco," said Agent Kirkwal. "To the family of George Shen. We sent a wire to the San Francisco police department, giving them the name and address on the driver's license."

"There's another piece of paper," said Kennelly. It was a typed letter, not on letterhead but on a plain sheet of paper—

Jan. 21, '43

Dear George,

Sorry I had to do this to you, kid, but Fred's illness left no one to cover the East, and I guess you know we can't expect to survive this tough year if we don't do a good business in the East. I figure you can get in a good three or four weeks working Wash., Philly, NY, Boston & Baltimore and still get back to SF in plenty of time for your wedding.

You'll remember at the sales meeting Doug put a lot of emphasis on 23-1424 and 23-1543. It turns out those items aren't selling so hot out here, so I'd work more on old standbys like 17-6555 and 17-7654. Men like the tried and true, I guess. On the ladies styles though you should push items like 23-3432 and 23-3433. Personally I couldn't believe the gals would go for those heels, but I guess something like that has special appeal in drab times.

I know I can count on you to hold up your end. I phoned Miss Chin and apologized for having to send you on this trip. Promised her you'd be back in plenty of time. You're a lucky guy, George—and I guess she's lucky too.

Let me have a report as soon as possible.

Ben

Mrs. Roosevelt shook her head. "Really most distressing," she said.

"Maybe," said Kennelly.

"Maybe?"

"I could feel a whole lot more sympathy about a poor little shoe salesman who got dead if I knew how he got into the White House tonight—and into the Map Room besides."

"Also if we knew what he was doing here," said Kirkwal.

"There is one more thing you have to know," Kennelly said to the First Lady. "Mr. Shen was carrying a gun—what's called a Baby Browning, a very small automatic."

Kennelly reached into his jacket pocket and pulled out the automatic, wrapped in a white handkerchief. He unwrapped it on a table and let Mrs. Roosevelt see the stubby little weapon, no more than four inches long.

She frowned hard. "This man has not only entered the White House," she said, "but has carried a gun to the second floor and to within thirty or forty feet of the door to the President's bedroom—and, for that matter, only half that distance to the door to Madame Chiang's suite."

"Not to mention that the man who killed him—"

Mrs. Roosevelt interrupted Kirkwal. "I am afraid we have to confront the possibility that he was killed by someone who did not have to enter the White House—by someone who was already here."

Kirkwal scowled. "The Chinese, you mean. Madame's staff."

"Maybe he came here to assassinate Madame Chiang," said Kennelly. "Maybe he was spotted by one of her staff, who immediately killed him."

"Not all of her people are very clearly defined," said Kirkwal. "One or more of them could be security agents or body-guards."

"Just how many does she have?" Kennelly asked. "And where are they. More to the point, where were they when this man was killed?"

"Exactly when *was* he killed, Mr. Kirk-wal?" asked Mrs. Roosevelt.

"The body was discovered by one of the White House policemen making his rounds," said Kirkwal. "He called in his report at 8:57. I think Dr. Gray can tell us something about how long the man had been dead."

The young doctor, who had remained timidly apart from the conversation, now nodded and said, "I arrived at 9:40, approximately. Judging from the coagulation of the blood and other factors— I mean, I palpated the muscles of the arms and legs to determine the degree of stiffening. Uh . . . I would judge the man had been dead approximately an hour, certainly not much more."

"Which matches what the policeman told us," said Kennelly. "He looked into this room about 8:12, maybe 8:15. Everything was normal. At 8:57 there was a body."

"So we need to know where people were during about forty minutes," said Mrs. Roosevelt.

"Exactly," said Kirkwal.

"Of Madame Chiang's staff, I can tell you where three were. Mr. Weng Guo-fang and Mr. and Miss Kung were at dinner with the President."

"How many more people are with her?" asked Kennelly.

"She has two maids," said Mrs. Roosevelt. "Plus a secretary: a young man. Plus a factotum."

"Where are all these people housed?" Kennelly asked.

"Madame Chiang occupies the Queen's Suite. Mr. Weng Guo-fang and Miss Kung are occupying two bedrooms within the private family quarters—rooms used by my daughter and sons and their families when they visit the White House.

Mr. Kung and the rest of Madame's staff are housed on the third floor."

"The maids are on duty at all times," said Kirkwal. "They are in the sitting room of the Queen's Suite, waiting for the call to the bedroom or bath. Weng Guo-fang asked that a White House maid be assigned to them, to bring their meals and so on. They've been told to use the telephone and call for what they want."

"The secretary and the factotum could be bodyguards," said Mrs. Roosevelt. "Even the maids could be. They could all be armed. When the Soviet foreign minister, Mr. Molotov, was here, he carried a big ugly revolver and kept it within reach when he was in bed at night."

"If I were Molotov," said Kennelly, "I'd have a pistol on me all the time."

"Shen's throat was not cut with a pistol," said Kirkwal. "It was cut with— With what, Doctor?"

"I'd guess a straight razor," said the doctor. "Something very sharp."

"From behind, do you think?" asked Mrs. Roosevelt.

"I don't know. We haven't undressed

him. When that's done, for the autopsy, we may find bruises that will be suggestive."

"Would cutting a man's throat require any great strength?" she asked.

"That depends on whether or not the man struggled. If he were surprised, the slashing through his throat, making a deep wound, would cut off his breath. Well . . . Actually, he might breathe through the wound for some little time, as blood sucked down as he inhaled filled his lungs. I would judge that Mr. Shen bled to death."

"A death struggle, at least," she said. "Does that not suggest that someone did something to him to keep him quiet while he died?"

"I examined him for a blow to the head. There was none."

Mrs. Roosevelt glanced around the room and sighed. "The carpet must be taken up immediately," she said to Kirkwal. "I mean, tonight. I don't mean to have the President wheel himself in here tomorrow morning and see—"

"Can we remove the body now?" the doctor asked.

"Take him into the West Sitting Hall

and down on the elevator. I am not sure how I can emphasize enough the necessity of keeping this matter confidential. To have it known that a Chinese-American was murdered in the White House during the visit of Madame Chiang Kai-shek would create a newspaper and radio carnival. Not only that, the lady might decide to flee the White House, saying it isn't safe."

"I believe we've done all we can do tonight, Ma'am," said Kirkwal. "May I suggest you try to get a good night's sleep?"

"Oh, yes. With visions of that poor man lying there in a pool of his own blood. Yes, I am certain I shall sleep well."

III

"Mr. President! Mr. Speaker! Madame Chiang Kai-shek!"

Speaker Rayburn rapped the gavel for order, but the Joint Session stood and gave the First Lady of China a standing ovation as the reception committee led her down the center aisle to the well, then to the dais, of the House of Representatives.

The senators and representatives of the committee appointed to receive her had not been chosen as the tallest members of Congress; but to the people on the floor and in the galleries, who could barely catch a glimpse of her in the midst of those towering men, it must have seemed they had been appointed to hide her.

Mrs. Roosevelt beamed from the gallery—though she had her reservations about the way the iron-willed lady from China would probably play to the emotions, not just of the Congress, but of the American people. She had already said one thing that could not be overlooked: that America had gone to war in 1941, not because of an attack by Hitler, but because of an attack by Japan, so many Americans felt that Japan was the chief enemy and must be defeated first. That was, of course, exactly what she and the Generalissimo wanted.

The tall, distinguished-looking Vice President of the United States, Henry A. Wallace, bent forward to say a word of personal greeting and welcome to Madame Chiang.

As always, the First Lady of China wore an ankle-length, slender dress of black silk, slit to her knees and just above on both sides, decorated with sewn-on chips of jade and a few glittering sequins. She smiled her acknowledgment of the applause. She stood behind a battery of microphones and stared back at the Congress: cold and hard as a jewel, confident that their applause was nothing more than she deserved.

Then she was introduced and began to speak.

She spoke first of the grand alliance of four "Great Powers," by which she meant the United States, Great Britain, the Soviet Union, and China. She talked about the "inevitable victory" of the "brave armies each of our great nations has committed to battle against lawless aggression." The Congress jumped to its feet to applaud—blissfully oblivious, apparently, of the fact that China was not a great power by any stretch of the imagination, that there was no real government in China, where her husband's writ ran only where he could enforce it, which wasn't far, and that his "brave armies" did not amount to even a tiny fraction of the three hundred divisions he claimed he commanded.

Asia, she said, was home to a majority of all the population of the world. The power that dominated Asia would dominate the world. A little more aid to China, now, would prevent Japanese domination. In fact, she said, she and her husband looked forward to a world in which no nation would be dominant, in which freely elected governments would honor each other's rights and live in peace.

She talked eloquently of a postwar world in which every man and woman would live in freedom, with dignity and justice.

Men and women in the audience who had experienced life under her husband's government whispered behind their hands that "Peanut" would not recognize freedom or justice if it sneaked up behind him and kicked him in the backside.

The Congress, even so, kept interrupting Madame Chiang with stormy applause.

Mrs. Roosevelt's feelings were mixed. She understood, first, that Madame Chiang was appealing to the American nation to override the decisions the President and the Prime Minister had made and to compel the alliance to reverse course. On the other hand, she had to admire the way a woman was dominating the Congress. Friends like Elinor Morgenthau had already warned her not to take seriously Madame Chiang's declarations of devotion to the cause of equality and justice, but she found it difficult to imagine that all this powerful eloquence was not backed by sincerity.

The President could. He was decidedly cold about the speech. He sent word to Mrs. Roosevelt that press of business would prevent his attending a luncheon for Madame Chiang and congressional leaders. He sent along a statement to be read. It was worded in slippery diplomatic terms, but it repeated his firm commitment to the Germany-first strategy he and Churchill had agreed on at Casablanca and before.

After lunch, Madame Chiang acknowledged herself tired and said she would take a nap.

The mystery of the murder in the Map Room had never been far from the front of the First Lady's thoughts, even when she was concentrating on Madame Chiang's speech. As soon as she could find a moment, she called Agent Robert Kirkwal and asked him to come to her study. He arrived in a few minutes.

"What word?" she asked. She had taken the minutes between her call to him and his arrival to make editorial marks on the draft of an article she was writing for *Collier's*. "Do we have any important new information?"

He sat down in the armchair beside her desk. "Some rather interesting facts," he said. "The murder victim was carrying a cyanide capsule in his mouth. It was concealed between his teeth and his cheek. He could have committed suicide at any moment."

"How singularly hideous!"

"Large bruises on his arms suggest that he was pinned from behind by one man while another cut his throat."

"Man— It could have been a woman. A man might have pinned him from behind, while a woman cut his throat."

"Possibly."

"Anyway, let us not *assume* it was a man."

Kirkwal nodded. "Continuing . . ." he said. "The State of California confirms the issuance of a driver's license to George C. Shen, 412 Sacramento Street, San Francisco, in September 1942. The address is that of a boardinghouse. So far, no family has been located."

"What of Miss Chin, his fiancée?"

"Chin is a common family name in San Francisco. There is no listing for a Chin Yu-lin, which suggests that she is the daughter of a Chin family and living at home. But which Chin family?"

"The Chin family that is having a wedding," said Mrs. Roosevelt. "I have a friend at the *San Francisco Chronicle*. I'll ask him to inquire of his society editor."

"All right. Shen was a salesman for a shoe company based in San Francisco—"

"We are not sure of that," said Mrs. Roosevelt. "The letter from 'Ben' included no suggestion as to where it was written. Mr. Shen seems not to have preserved the envelope. He may have received that letter from anywhere."

Robert Kirkwal at first frowned, then smiled, and finally grinned. "In that case, Ed Kennelly has some men out on a wild-goose chase. He sent two detectives, or maybe three, out to ask shoe stores around town if they bought shoes from a San Francisco company, then get its name, and so on."

"What they should be asking is whether or not they have had calls from an Oriental salesman."

Yes. Of course . . . Shen was new in this territory, replacing the sick 'Fred.' He may not be known to—"

"Knowing what we now know of him, it is not unlikely he made *no* sales calls, that he was not a shoe salesman at all."

"I very much doubt he was," said Kirkwal.

"Even so, it would be worthwhile for Captain Kennelly's men to continue their inquiry, asking the right questions. Perhaps Mr. Shen was a shoe salesman, after all—with a sideline, as we might call it."

"Actually, it's very likely he had a cover," said Kirkwal.

"That is, if he was a spy."

She realized that was the first time the word *spy* had come into the talk about the murder of George Shen. She had thought that was what he might have been, from the moment she learned that he was dead in the Map Room; but the word had not passed from thought to voice until now.

Kirkwal realized it, too. Interjection of the word changed the parameters of the investigation.

Mrs. Roosevelt shook her head. "Let's try not to talk of this case in terms of espionage. I believe you can understand why."

"If we do," said Kirkwal grimly, "we

can hardly keep the FBI out of the investigation."

"And we do not wish to have . . ." She stopped, cutting off a word that was in her mind. "We do not wish to have Mr. John Edgar Hoover conducting an investigation inside the White House."

"I quite understand and quite agree," said Kirkwal. "We need not explain it to each other."

"What have you done toward discovering how the man got into the White House?" she asked.

"The officer in charge of the military guard is Major John Bentz. We had to take him into our confidence, of course. I don't see how we could have avoided that."

"You couldn't. Anyway, Major Bentz is to be trusted. He worked with Mr. Baines and Sir Alan Burton on the pantry murders, during the Prime Minister's visit in December of 1941."

"He is interrogating his men who were on the gates last night," said Kirkwal.

"Let him not limit his inquiry to them," she said. "He has men in antiaircraft batteries on the grounds and on the roof.

They are in positions to observe a great deal, *if* they are observant."

Mrs. Roosevelt pushed back her chair, rose, and walked to the window. She looked out on the Ellipse, the Washington Monument, and, beyond, the new Jefferson Memorial. She was glad they had been able to complete and dedicate the monument to Thomas Jefferson, in spite of the war. A light snow was falling. That was how it usually was in Washington in February: light, wet snow or cold rain. If she had to see snow, she wished she could see the deep, crackling snow of the Hudson Valley or New England.

"I imagine Washington is not your original home, Mr. Kirkwal," she said.

"My accent . . ."

"You don't talk like a native Virginian or Marylander."

Kirkwal grinned. "No one in the rest of the civilized world speaks English like a Marylander," he said.

"But who speaks as you do?"

"Londoners," he said. "I was fourteen years old when my father decided we were moving to the States. By that time it was too late for me. I shall always speak as I did when I lived in Stepney."

"Stepney . . . You are fortunate you did not live there during the Blitz."

"A sister and two cousins," said Kirkwal.

"Oh, I'm *sorry,* Mr. Kirkwal."

"My sister was eighteen and married when my father brought me to the States. She stayed. She had two sons in the forces. Both are still living, so far as I know. The cousins . . . Well, I didn't know them. Never met them. And the old place where we lived— The house." He shrugged. "No great loss. But I tell you, I don't take it very kindly of Madame Chiang to want us to switch the focus of the war to Asia."

"I think you need not worry much about that," said Mrs. Roosevelt. "That is, of course, strictly between us. You are a naturalized citizen, then?"

"Yes, Ma'am. I'm forty-four years old, just a bit too old for our forces or British forces. Otherwise . . ."

"And how long have you been with the Secret Service?"

"Since 1925, Ma'am. Eighteen years. Some of it protecting the vice presidents."

"Mr. Kirkwal . . . You need not interject 'ma'am' into every other sentence. I appreciate the courtesy, but it is awkward between two people holding protracted conversation."

"Ah. Thank you. I'm called 'Bobby,' incidentally. Bobby Kirkwal. Feel welcome."

"Oddly, I have never called the agents who protect us anything but Mr. This and Mr. That. Maybe— Well. Anyway, you need not call me 'ma'am.'"

"When I was a lad," he said, "being called 'mister' made a fellow think he was a toff."

Mrs. Roosevelt laughed. "Well, you are one now—in the better sense."

"Thank you."

"So. How old did the medical examiner think Mr. Shen was? I mean, did he think the driver's license was accurate in describing him as forty-one years old?"

"I saw no comment on that. The autopsy report will say 'early forties,' I believe."

"Does it occur to you that Mr. Shen obtained his driver's license rather late in life?" she asked. "And, what is more, is it not odd that he should have obtained his license in wartime, when cars and gasoline are scarce? Does the State of California have any record indicating that this was Mr. Shen's first license? In other words, did he take a test, or did he obtain his license on the basis of an earlier license obtained in another state?"

"What does that imply, do you think?"

"I don't know, but I think it's an interesting circumstance."

"We agree, I suppose," said Kirkwal, "that we are unlikely to find out who killed Shen until we find out who Shen was."

"And why he was in the White House," she added.

"And how he got in."

"There are enough lines of inquiry to keep several investigators busy," said Mrs. Roosevelt.

"Yes. I'm glad we have Ed Kennelly."

"He has always been helpful. Oh, and . . . So far as I know, there has been no inquiry from reporters."

"I think we managed to get the body out of the White House without anybody the wiser," said Kirkwal.

"I hope the men who attend to the maps like their new carpet," said the First Lady.

The dinner for the second night of the visit of Madame Chiang Kai-shek was more formal—and, as Henrietta Nesbitt, the White House housekeeper put it— more formidable. It was Mrs. Nesbitt who had to manage ration points to keep food on the White House tables, she who had to serve the Roosevelts and guests their meals within a strictly limited budget; and the demands of the First Lady of China, for herself and her staff, had cut deeply into Mrs. Nesbitt's available money and points—all of this besides the demands for extra maids, irons, ironing boards, towels, soap, incense, hot plates, teapots . . .

To assuage the testy housekeeper a little, Mrs. Roosevelt had arranged for her to have a ticket to the gallery, to watch Madame Chiang deliver her speech to Congress that morning. Mrs. Nesbitt had shrugged and harrumphed when Mrs. Roosevelt asked her what she thought of the speech. "She uses words I never even heard of."

Among the guests for tonight's black-tie dinner was Wendell Willkie: he, the fifty-year-old "adolescent," in Madame Chiang's assessment. Mrs. Roosevelt wondered if the President would manage to restrain himself tonight or would somehow amuse himself with a circular reference to what China's First Lady had said of Willkie.

Besides Willkie, tonight's guests included Secretary of State Cordell Hull; Secretary of War Henry Stimson; General George C. Marshall, Army Chief of Staff; Admiral Ernest King, Chief of Naval Operations; Senator Arthur Vandenberg of Michigan; and Senator Harry Truman of Missouri.

The guest list included a significant omission.

It was Henry Luce. Madame Chiang had suggested she would be pleased to see Henry Luce—"the most distinguished of American publishers"—at the dinner. The President had balked at that.

These and other tensions underlay the evening. Some of the guests were aware of them.

Once again, Madame Chiang Kai-shek appeared in black: this time with more jade and sequins sewed to her black silk. Weng Guo-fang again wore colorful silk, in the manner of an old Mandarin. Mr. and Miss Kung appeared in tuxedoes.

Cocktails were served in the small dining room, where dinner had been served last night. Dinner would be served in the State Dining Room.

The seventy-six-year-old Henry L. Stimson was an imposing figure in the administration. He was a prestigious New York lawyer, to begin with; but, more to the point, he had served as Secretary of War for two years in the administration of President William Howard Taft, as Secretary of State throughout the administration of President Herbert Hoover, and as President Roosevelt's Secretary of War since July 1940. He was an imposing figure in appearance, too—tall, slender, grave of expression, with strong gray hair and a gray mustache.

Madame Chiang knew him as a puissant adviser to the President: a man whose views were never dismissed lightly. Besides, he had also served as Governor-

General of the Philippines and knew more than most American statesmen about the politics of Asia. Madame Chiang recognized the importance of Henry Stimson, and she made a point of approaching him at the cocktail hour and, in effect, attaching herself to him.

The President, sitting in his wheelchair, apparently without a care in the world except to entertain and enjoy his friends, cast a significant glance toward the First Lady, which from experience she interpreted as meaning "Keep close to that and listen." She joined Mr. Stimson and Madame Chiang just in time to hear the First Lady of China say—

"I imagine, truth be known, that we share a wide circle of friends and acquaintances."

"Probably we do," said Stimson. He held a cigar in his left hand, a glass of Scotch in his right, and he nodded gravely. "Probably we do." He said it thoughtfully, but Mrs. Roosevelt had learned of Henry Stimson that he was a master of understatement, or—more correctly said—of meaningless and noncommittal statements.

"We've both lived in America, in the same circles."

"I regret that you have never lived in China," said Madame Chiang.

"I regret that I have never had the opportunity to expand my experience and understanding by living in a number of places where it might have been pleasant and instructive to live."

"General Stilwell is a disappointment," said Madame Chiang.

"War produces many of those," said Stimson.

"Are you disappointed with him, Mr. Secretary?"

"No, not really."

"Is the President disappointed with him?"

"I am not aware of the President's feelings about General Stilwell. I imagine he is satisfied with him."

Mrs. Roosevelt could hear Stimson's voice hardening. She wondered if Madame Chiang was perceptive enough to hear it, too. What Madame Chiang was pressing was her side of an argument that had been going on for some time: whether the best strategy for the war in China was the ground assault favored by General Joseph Stilwell or the air strategy favored by General Claire Chennault. To add to the difficulty, the Generalissimo and Madame Chiang personally disliked General Stilwell—a dislike thoroughly reciprocated by the general who in private called Chiang Kai-shek "Peanut." Secretary Stimson and General Marshall backed Stilwell.

Madame Chiang *was* perceptive. She frowned, then quickly smiled and said, "Do you know, Mr. Stimson, that you have the most beautiful hands?"

Stimson blushed. "Huh-huh," he laughed nervously. "Why . . . thank you," he said.

Madame Chiang nodded at the Secretary of War. "A deserved compliment, Mr. Stimson," she said. "Ah. There is Mr. Willkie. I must say hello to him."

Wendell Willkie stood beside the President's wheelchair and was smiling and talking with much animation. A moment ago his hearty laugh had rung out across the room. The President grinned and beamed. They had just shared something that obviously amused both of them.

Madame Chiang's comment that

Willkie was an adolescent was not entirely inappropriate, so far as his personal appearance was concerned—though entirely inappropriate with respect to the man's character and ability, in Mrs. Roosevelt's judgment. Willkie was a liberal Republican. The President had come to admire him— with reservations. They had become friends. From time to time Willkie was invited to the White House, where he met privately with the President, who was glad to have his views on a variety of issues.

Still, he did look boyish. His enthusiasm for the moment, for every moment, never diminished and was never hidden. His shaggy brown hair would never stay in place, except maybe with a heavy shot of the hair oil that he refused to pour on it. His big, square face was usually flushed, as it was tonight. Often his face gleamed with tiny beads of perspiration.

"Madame Chiang!" he said with a broad smile and conspicuously genuine pleasure. "It is good to see you again."

"It is splendid to see you again, Mr. Willkie," she said. "You look very fine. In good health, I trust."

"Younger and more robust every year,

Madame," said Willkie. "Give me another ten years, and I shall revert to my childhood."

Mrs. Roosevelt understood—and likely as not Madame Chiang did, too—that the President had told Willkie what Madame had said. Probably that had been the occasion for the big laugh a few minutes ago.

"I'm looking forward to a long talk with you, Mr. Willkie," said Madame Chiang. "I would like to enlist your support in winning congressional Republicans to back more assistance to China."

Mrs. Roosevelt all but gasped aloud. It was a cruel cut. Madame Chiang knew perfectly well that Wendell Willkie had almost no friends among congressional Republicans. He had never, in fact, been the leader of the Republican Party—only its candidate for President after his supporters stampeded the 1940 convention. The First Lady wondered what Madame Chiang had decided she held against Wendell Willkie.

He was not defenseless. "China is already receiving far more assistance than its contribution to winning the war merits," he said bluntly. "I am afraid I cannot accommodate you."

"I am grateful that very few Americans share your point of view," said Madame Chiang coldly.

"Nearly everyone who has the facts shares it," said Willkie.

"You must excuse me," said Madame Chiang. "I haven't spoken to General Marshall."

The President, who had thoroughly enjoyed the sharp little exchange, tried to hide his grin behind his martini glass.

"A most instructive conversation," said Mrs. Roosevelt quietly.

State dinners did not last late. Still, it was nearly eleven when the First Lady returned to her study in the private quarters on the second floor. She found on her desk a telephone note written by her secretary, Malvina Thompson, saying that she could call Mr. Kirkwal as late as midnight.

He came to her study a few minutes later, accompanied by Captain Kennelly.

"I know Captain Kennelly's marital

status," she said. "But you, Mr. Kirkwal . . . Don't you have a wife who objects to your working past midnight?"

"You must forgive me," said Kirkwal. "She is the only person to whom I have confided that there was a murder in the White House last night."

"Have you had dinner?"

"Indeed we have," said Kirkwal. "Not only that. We found the key to Mrs. Nesbitt's liquor cabinet and have enjoyed some first-rate whiskey."

"I should be glad to have coffee and brandy brought up," she said.

"I hope we can finish our business and go home to bed—allowing you to retire, too—in just a few minutes."

"Well, then. Have you learned something?"

"Ed—"

Kennelly nodded. "A thing or two," he said. "I suggested to Bobby that, while everybody was downstairs for the state dinner, he and I take the lock apart. I mean, the lock on the Map Room door. Which we did."

"With what result?"

"You can't be sure," said Kennelly.

"But the insides of that lock are all covered with scratches. I'd say it was *picked.*"

"With what?" asked Mrs. Roosevelt.

"An interesting question," said Kennelly. "Mr. Shen didn't have a tool on him. Which means one of two things—either someone besides Shen picked the lock, or someone took the pick off his body after he killed him."

"We know, of course, that at least two intruders were in the Map Room. That is to say, Mr. Shen was there and whoever killed him was there."

"There could have been more," said Kirkwal. "There could have been a whole . . . platoon of them."

"Doing what?"

"Looking at the situation maps, we have to assume," said Kirkwal. "What else?"

"They don't display any great secrets," said Mrs. Roosevelt.

"Well, one more bit of information before we go on speculating," said Kennelly. "I had the two letters dusted for fingerprints. I mean, the letter signed 'Yu-lin' and the one signed 'Ben.' They had fingerprints on them. Shen's, of course, on both of them. Then two other sets, apparently 'Ben's' and 'Yu-lin's.' I had those run through the FBI files. Nothing. Neither 'Ben' or 'Yu-lin' has ever been fingerprinted—that is, never that produced an FBI record."

"What about Mr. Shen?"

"No fingerprints on file. He registered for the draft, though, from the same address, on Sacramento Street. That was in 1940."

"The San Francisco police are giving us good cooperation," said Kirkwal.

"Even so," said Kennelly, "we're not finding out much. We've had no success in locating a Chinese shoe salesman—not one who sold shoes in Washington, anyway. I've asked Philadelphia, New York, and Boston to ask the shoe stores in their towns."

"How far will they go?"

"Well . . . Maybe a dozen stores apiece. We really can't ask the NYPD to inquire of every shoe store in New York."

"No. Well, gentlemen," said the First Lady with a warm smile, "it *is* late, isn't it? I must sit in on a news conference in the morning."

"I'd rather be lookin' for a murderer," said Kennelly.

IV

The press would indeed assemble for a news conference with Madame Chiang Kai-Shek, in mid-morning. Mrs. Roosevelt's day began with something very different.

Lieutenant Commander Joshua Gregg, skipper of a submarine operating in the waters just north of Guadalcanal, had remained alone on the conning tower, firing a machine gun at an approaching Japanese gunboat, until he was wounded and fell. Knowing Japanese airplanes were approaching, he ordered the crew to dive the boat, even though he remained outside and would inevitably drown. This morning the President was awarding him the Congressional Medal of Honor, posthumously.

Jane Gregg, his widow, and Josh, his son, were the First Lady's guests for breakfast in the private dining room. Frank

Knox, Secretary of the Navy, would join them.

Jane Gregg was an exceptionally beautiful young woman. She wore her blond hair long and smooth, and this morning it was partially bound under a blue rayon scarf. Her lipstick was glaring red. She wore a tailored jacket and skirt, both dark blue.

The little boy was seven. He was dressed in a gray suit, white shirt, and necktie.

There were few occasions on which Mrs. Roosevelt found it difficult to control her emotions. This was one of them. She embraced Jane Gregg, then sat down and lifted the little boy on her lap. Only with difficulty did she control her voice and hold back her tears.

"Do you want to be a naval officer, like your father?" Frank Knox asked the little boy.

He nodded.

Knox spoke to Jane Gregg. "You know, he has an automatic appointment to Annapolis, if he wants it. The sons of Medal of Honor winners are in a special category."

"Thank you," the young woman said. "I didn't know that."

"Is there anything we can do for you, my dear?" Mrs. Roosevelt asked.

"Everyone has been very kind."

The First Lady turned to Josh. "Do you like orange juice?" she asked.

He shook his head.

"Bacon and eggs?"

He shook his head.

"What would you like for breakfast?"

"Rice Crispies," said the little boy.

At last Mrs. Roosevelt could smile. "You shall have Rice Crispies," she said. She summoned the waiter standing a little away from the table. "Won't he?"

"Yes, *Ma'am.* I know there's a box of 'em in the pantry. We'll have 'em up here in two minutes."

"Good. Now, Josh, since you are going to have your Rice Crispies, do you suppose a glass of orange juice might taste good while the man goes to get them?"

The little boy nodded and picked up his glass.

The First Lady spoke to Jane Gregg. "I wonder if my boys still yearn for their favorite cereals at breakfast. I know Elliott found it very difficult to confront smoked fish across an English breakfast table."

Three quarters of an hour later, the President hung the medal around the young widow's neck, in the Oval Office. A White House photographer took a picture of the brief ceremony. Jane Gregg wept— which was why she had asked that reporters not be allowed in. So, then, did Mrs. Roosevelt. And the President himself put aside his prince-nez and wiped his eyes.

Half an hour remained before the press conference for Madame Chiang Kai-shek. Mrs. Roosevelt asked Frank Knox if he could spare her a few minutes, and when he said he could she led him to the second floor and to her study.

"Mr. Secretary," she said, "I wonder if I could speak with you in great confidence?"

"Of course," said the Secretary of the Navy.

She knew she could trust him. Like Stimson, Knox was a prominent Republican. The President had appointed them

Secretary of War and Secretary of the Navy to give his wartime administration a bipartisan quality. The President had chosen Knox, a prominent newspaperman, because he knew him as a Republican of moderate and internationalist views. He had served with Teddy Roosevelt's Rough Riders and had bolted the party when the Colonel bolted in 1912. He had won the President's respect and had served very effectively in his wartime post.

"I should like," she said, "to have two letters delivered to you. They are at present at District police headquarters, where they have been examined for fingerprints. There is some reason to believe that the person from whose . . . body they were taken was a spy. That may be fanciful, but there is some reason to believe it. It has so far proved impossible to verify the origins of these two letters. So it has occurred to me that they may have been coded messages."

"From whom? Do you have any idea?"

"No. They were taken from a Chinese-American who was murdered Wednesday evening. It occurred to me that the Department of the Navy has a highly skilled cryptanalytic service and that one of your analysts might be able to find a hidden meaning in these letters."

"I'd be happy to submit them to our cryptanalysts and see what we can find out."

"I should be grateful. I shall have the letters delivered to you as soon as possible."

During the press conference, Madame Chiang continued her effort to win public opinion to her point of view. She was very good at it, too, Mrs. Roosevelt observed. Alternately imploring and demanding, somber and witty, outgoing and withdrawn, she overwhelmed the normally cynical White House reporters, many of whom were already sympathetic toward her or were under orders from their publishers to be sympathetic.

"A very small amount of additional aid to China now," she said, "will make it possible for us to move against Japan with the power of three hundred army divisions."

No one questioned her statement. No

one seemed to realize that the Generalissimo did not command thirty divisions, much less three hundred.

The press conference had exhausted her, she said. Without taking lunch, she returned to the Queen's Suite and went to bed.

Major John Bentz accompanied Mrs. Roosevelt and Agent Robert Kirkwal on a walk around the White House grounds.

"We have tightened security a great deal since December 1941," said Major Bentz.

Mrs. Roosevelt observed that the major, whom she spoke with only very infrequently, had aged in the past fifteen months. He had been boyish when she first met him. Now he was a more mature-looking man. He no longer wore a Sam Browne belt or carried a riding crop. He wore an overseas cap and, today, an olive-drab raincoat. She suspected he was not pleased with his assignment as commander of the White House security detail. He would win no medals here, and maybe no promotions.

He pointed at a heavy steel grating. "You remember we welded that shut after Mr. Deconcini and Commander Leach went through the tunnel," he said. "We've found some other gaps since. They're welded shut, too—either literally or figuratively."

"We are thinking in terms of three people, Major," said Mrs. Roosevelt. "Mr. Shen and the two who killed him. Have you no idea how they could have entered the White House?"

"Ma'am . . . My guess would be they didn't enter; they were already inside."

The First Lady shook her head. "Not Mr. Shen. He was not a member of Madame Chiang's staff. He certainly was not a member of the White House staff. Even if we accept the thought that he was killed by someone who had legitimate access to the premises, Mr. Shen did not, and must have somehow entered."

"Through our security," said Major Bentz grimly.

"I am afraid so," said Mrs. Roosevelt.

"It is frustrating," she said a little later to Kirkwal and Kennelly as they sat in the

Map Room. "After two days, almost, we don't even know the identity of the victim."

"I've been reading the autopsy report again," said Kennelly. "There's something in it I overlooked before. Look—"

He handed over a copy of the report, bearing a checkmark in pencil in the margin of the second page.

✔ The alcohol content of the subject's blood, by volume, is .17%. The subject may, therefore, be regarded as having been moderately inebriated at the time of death. Also, a trace of codeine or morphine was found, suggesting that the subject had ingested a small quantity of one of these compounds within the 72 hours immediately preceding his death.

"Odd condition for a man who had just somehow managed to enter the White House, through tight security, and make his way to the Map Room," said Kennelly.

They were alone in the Map Room. The two officers charged with constantly updating the situation maps were away from the White House. They would return and mark the maps one more time for this date, about five o'clock.

The Map Room did not afford the President nearly as much information as he could get in the Situation Room on the ground floor, but it was convenient for him. He could wheel himself in and stare at the maps as he read the reports of action in the South Pacific or in North Africa or the Soviet Union—indeed, anywhere in the world.

Maps hung from the walls and stood on easels. The information on them differed from information on the maps in the Situation Room in one very significant way. The ones in the Situation Room carried marks indicating planned future moves by Allied forces. The ones here only showed present positions: information the enemy certainly had, too.

It was this that Mrs. Roosevelt had in mind when she said, as she had said before, "Why in the world the Map Room?"

"Maybe he was too drunk to know where he was," Kirkwal suggested.

"I doubt that," said Kennelly. "Under the law of most states, you can legally drive a car if your blood alcohol does not exceed

.15%. Some states have lowered that to .10%, and there's a campaign to lower it everywhere. But if you can drive a car with .1499% in you, then you will know where you are when you have .17%."

"In any case, Captain Kennelly, wouldn't you regard the man with .17% as drunk?" asked Mrs. Roosevelt.

"I certainly would," said Kennelly. "Not blind, staggering drunk but certainly impaired, as the word is."

"Are we saying, then, that a drunk worked his way through White House security and made his way to the second floor, unnoticed?"

"With help," said Kirkwal ominously. "He didn't *get* in. Someone *let* him in. It has to be."

"Assuming that is so," said Mrs. Roosevelt, "did the same person or persons let in the ones who killed him?"

"Or did *they* kill him?" asked Kennelly.

"Captain Kennelly, you have before indulged my penchant for making charts of our facts. May I—?"

"Please do," he said. "They have always been helpful."

She removed one of the maps from

an easel and uncovered a large tablet of blank sheets. "As a beginning," she said, starting to scribble with a crayon—

KNOWN

1. Death occurred between 8:12 and 8:57 P.M.
2. At least two persons were involved.
3. Victim was inebriated.
4. Victim was known as George Shen since at least September 1942, when he got a driver's license.
5. Map Room lock was picked.
6. No one yet identified saw when Shen in WH. (But <u>someone</u> saw him.)

UNKNOWN

1. Identity and business of Shen.
2. His reason for being in WH.
3. Who killed him?
4. Why?

"A point," said Kirkwal. "During the 8:12 to 8:57 time period, White House security was focused on the first floor, where the President and First Lady, plus Madame Chiang and her party were having dinner. I don't mean to suggest the second floor was not protected, but it has secondary priority when the people the Secret Service must protect are elsewhere in the White House."

"You have limited personnel," said Mrs. Roosevelt. "The Congress has consistently declined to appropriate money for more protection."

"There was a man on duty in the West Sitting Hall, just outside the President's study. Another man was on duty in the East Hall, to protect the Queen's Suite."

"To protect Madame Chiang."

"Yes. As demanded by Mr. Weng Guo-fang. He made a strong point when he arrived that Madame's suite must be guarded at all times. Since service stairs come up in the East Hall, the man who guards that suite must stick pretty close to the door."

Mrs. Roosevelt wrote a seventh fact under her list of KNOWNs: "Map Room not specifically guarded."

Ed Kennelly scowled and ground his right fist in his left palm. "We'll get nowhere on this until we find out who George C. Shen was."

"I am inclined to agree," said Mrs. Roosevelt.

A box full of letters to be answered sat on the First Lady's desk. Malvina "Tommy" Thompson, her secretary, sat in a chair with her shorthand pad on her lap, while Mrs. Roosevelt scanned the letters— all of which she had already read—and dictated answers.

She shook her head. "Another 'Eleanor Club' complaint," she said. "Send the usual letter—'To the best of my knowledge there is no such thing as an Eleanor Club. If there is, such was formed without my consent.' Et cetera. I—"

She was interrupted by the ringing of the telephone.

Tommy picked it up. "Mr. Greschner," she said quietly, cupping her hand over the mouthpiece.

Mrs. Roosevelt took the telephone. "Ed? How very nice of you to call."

Edward Greschner was the publisher of the *San Francisco Chronicle*.

"Well, it was good to talk to you yesterday," he said. "I asked around about your man George Shen and his fiancée, Miss Chin. I've come up with a little information."

"About Miss Chin?"

"No. About Shen, actually. But, to dispose of the problem of Miss Chin—my society editor has no information about a wedding coming up for the daughter of any Chin family. Of course, you have to remember we might not have the information. The Chinese families don't usually care much whether we publish their society news or not. I called a couple of Chinese editors. They've got nothing on it, either."

"Does that impress you as at all odd?"

"Not really. It would impress me as odd if the wedding had already taken place and they hadn't placed a story about it. But many times they don't bother sending in a story in advance."

"But you have learned something about Mr. Shen?"

"Yes. Something you may find useful. I sent a reporter to the address on Sacramento Street. It's a rooming house. Shen lived there for two or three years and moved out about the first of the year. They had no forwarding address for him. He seems to be a bit mysterious. But he has no police record out here, not with the San Francisco Police Department or with the state."

"Did anyone confirm that he was a shoe salesman?"

"To the contrary, they said he worked for Occident and Orient Steamship Lines. At least, he told them he had—until December 1941. Until December seventh, O and O ships still called at Yokohama and Osaka, carried freight and passengers between the West Coast and Japan. Shen said he worked as an interpreter in the O and O offices."

"Interpreter? Japanese?"

"So he said. And there seems to have been a confirmation of it. In February last year army MPs arrested him at the rooming house and were going to carry him off to one of the camps where we've got the Nisei Japanese interned. Some patriot at the steamship offices turned him in, apparently—figured if he could speak Japanese he *was* Japanese. He had to prove he was Chinese."

"How did he do that?"

"Documentation. That's what he told the other roomers when he came back. He said he'd shown the authorities his grandparents' immigration records."

"But he lost his job, just the same?"

"Well . . . O and O doesn't sail to Japan anymore. In fact, nearly all their ships have been pressed into government service."

"Did Mr. Shen tell anyone how he came to speak Japanese?"

"No. The people at the rooming house describe him as pretty much a loner who never got much notice until the day when he was arrested. Afterward, when he was released, he explained what had happened. That was the most conversation anyone there ever had with him."

"Most interesting . . . Is there anything more?"

"His fellow roomers, as many as are left from the days when he lived in the house, describe him as moody. They say he sat in his room and drank some evenings. He never got drunk, not in any obnoxious sense, but he took on a lot of whiskey."

"This is most helpful, Ed. I cannot explain *how* helpful."

"I'll look to you to explain when you think you can," he said. "And I'll keep on it out here. If I learn anything more, I'll call."

"Thank you so very much."

Putting the telephone down, Mrs. Roosevelt's mind made a quick switch. " 'Eleanor Clubs,' " she said. "How many letters this week?"

"Thirty-one," said Tommy Thompson. "Not as many as last week."

"I know how these things get started," said the First Lady. "What I don't know is how to stop them."

"You can't," said Tommy. "You just have to let them die of their own accord."

They were talking about the latest vicious anti-Roosevelt story that was being told all over the country but particularly in the South. The rumor was that Negro domestic servants, especially cooks, were forming themselves into "Eleanor Clubs" and would, on a signal from the White House, all quit their jobs. The clubs were supposed to have a slogan: "Put the white woman back in the kitchen in '43."

"I am never so much distressed that

nasty people would hatch such lies as I am that some innocent people will believe them."

"You can never go wrong underestimating the intelligence of what Mencken calls *boobus Americanus,*" said Tommy.

"Oh, I can't be that cynical," said Mrs. Roosevelt. "Surely, though, the women who have written to us must realize that if thousands and thousands of Negro women quit their jobs, those Negro women would suffer from the loss of income. How *can—?*"

"Did you ever listen to a southern woman talk about her cook or housekeeper?" Tommy asked. "I have. 'Oh, Melinda, she's not like them other niggers. Why, I'd trust her with my *laaf!* She ain't like your run-of-the-mill niggers.' "

"Tommy . . ."

"They talk like that. Forgive me, but you can be naive sometimes. As you are about the Dragon Lady, if you will allow me to tell you."

"Madame Chiang?"

"She's a viper."

"She is the wife of the head of state of one of the great powers allied in this war."

"Nevertheless, she's a viper," said Tommy firmly. "I don't trust her."

The woman Tommy Thompson did not trust lay in a great tub of steaming water in the big bathroom of the Queen's Suite. Reclining and submerged up to her neck, she smoked a dark brown cigarette in a stubby amber holder. A cup of strong tea sat within her reach on a board across the tub. A glass of Napoleon brandy was also within reach.

Scattered around the bathroom were jars of creams and salves. Her maids had massaged her for most of an hour, as she lay on a padded massage table brought into the bathroom for the purpose. Looking youthful in her forties, she meant to preserve at least the veneer of youth, so far anyway as creams and massage could preserve it. Only after everything had its chance to penetrate her skin had she lowered herself into the water and demanded the hot-water tap be turned on to make her bath hotter.

Now, heavy-lidded, looking as if she

might go to sleep, she smoked her cigarette and sipped tea and brandy.

Suddenly she clapped her hands. "Miss Kung," she said.

The bathroom door opened, and Miss Kung, who had been waiting close to the door for her summons, entered.

The diminutive young woman was not dressed in her man's suit. No. She was stark naked. So were the maids. When Madame Chiang was naked, as she was in her bath, no one entered her presence who was not as naked as she.

General Stillwell called Chiang Kai-shek "Peanut." The literate members of Madame Chiang's staff had their scornful nickname for her. It was "Cleopatra."

Madame Chiang drew in smoke from her cigarette, then blew it out. "I want you to encrypt a message for the Generalissimo," she said. "It should read, 'The President will do anything I ask. I need not press him much about support. Our friends in Congress will take care of that. I propose to demand another Big Power meeting—Roosevelt, Churchill, and yourself. This will make it clear to the world that you are as important as any of them.' " She lifted her brandy to her lips but paused for a second to ask, "Do you have that?"

Miss Kung did not take shorthand or any kind of notes. She had trained herself to memorize the great lady's letters and messages. She nodded.

"Then send in the Little Father."

Miss Kung bowed and left the bathroom. Weng Guo-fang waited outside. She nodded toward the door, and he entered the bathroom.

Weng Guo-fang was the only man allowed to enter the presence of the Madame clothed when she was naked. Every servant knew it. What none of them knew was that he had been a servant to the Empress Dowager and was a eunuch.

The President served cocktails *en famille*—as he put it—that Friday evening. Dinner would be informal, served in the several suites, except for Mrs. Roosevelt's; and she had invited any of the Chinese party who wished to join her to the Private Dining Room for a buffet. She would be leaving, she told everyone, for a special event to sell war bonds, no later than seven o'clock.

Madame Chiang did not elect to appear. No one elected to give any reason why not. It was assumed she was experiencing some pain and weakness, still recovering from the surgery she had undergone in New York. Mr. Kung and Miss Kung appeared. So did Harry Hopkins and his wife. And, after the first round of drinks had already been consumed, so did Weng Guo-fang, this time wearing one of his fine gray suits.

"Mrs. Roosevelt," he said with a small and formal bow after he had picked up a glass of sherry and they stood a little apart from the others. "Would you be so kind as to put to rest a rumor that has come to our attention?"

"If I can."

He bowed again. "We have some reason to believe," he said quietly, with a polite little smile, "that an . . . untoward incident occurred in the White House, and not far from the doors to our agreeable accommodations, on Wednesday evening. Can you shed any light on this?"

Mrs. Roosevelt drew a quick, surprised breath—and hoped he did not notice. "Yes," she said. "A small matter. It involved unauthorized entry. It was quickly taken care of. There was no danger to anyone. Armed men stood between Madame Chiang's suite and the intruder. Also between your own rooms and the intruder."

"Have you identified this . . . intruder?"

"I don't know," she said. "It's a matter for the Secret Service and District police. I am sure they are handling it correctly."

Weng Guo-fang bowed again. "I am grateful for the assurance," he said.

As she had said she would do, Mrs. Roosevelt left the White House at seven, on her way to the Mayflower Hotel, where in the ballroom an auction was being held to sell war bonds.

By the time she arrived, hundreds of people were already milling around, looking at the items that would be put on sale. A huge banner hung across one end of the big room—

★ BUY BONDS! ★

Everything to be sold had been donated. Bids were to be in terms of war
bond purchases. Among the items donated were—

—A violin Jack Benny had played on
his radio show. He called it "Old Love in
Bloom."

—A twisted pool cue donated by
W. C. Fields.

—A derby hat from Stan Laurel and
another from Oliver Hardy.

—A pair of dancing shoes she had
worn in *The Wizard of Oz,* donated by
Judy Garland.

—A .44 caliber pistol carried by Wallace Beery in *Viva Villa!*

—A snap-brim fedora from Bud Abbot
and a pork-pie hat from Lou Costello.

—An autographed copy of the Cecil
Beaton photograph of Mrs. Roosevelt visiting the Royal Family in Buckingham Palace a few months ago.

All of these donors were present and
would be on the stage when their items
were auctioned. Hundreds of other items

were to be auctioned, donated by people who would not be present.

The master of ceremonies and auctioneer was Fred Allen.

Mrs. Roosevelt, who had immensely enjoyed *The Wizard of Oz,* was especially interested in having a few words with Judy Garland. She was a little surprised to find herself talking, not with a girl, but with a young woman of twenty-one, with a tense, edgy expression and a full figure, dressed in the "patriotic" style—that is, in an above-the-knees skirt that was supposed to save fabric, and bare legs since stockings were very scarce. She was far more surprised to smell the fumes of alcohol on the young woman's breath.

"You've grown up since 'Dorothy,' " said Mrs. Roosevelt.

"I was seventeen when I was 'Dorothy,' " said Judy Garland in her trademark throaty voice.

W. C. Fields walked over and joined them. He gave Judy Garland a familiar little pat on the rear.

"Oh, *Bill!*" she complained playfully.

"Mrs. Arrrr . . ." said Fields. "A pleasure indeeeed."

"It's good to meet you, Mr. Fields."

Fields, too, had been drinking—though with him it was no surprise. His face was flushed. His nose was swollen and red. His gray suit looked as if he had taken a nap in it.

"Beware of this one," Fields said, nodding at Judy Garland. "She drinks like a trooperrrr. I mean a cavalry trooperrrr. Which at her age, she shouldn't doooo. It's the studio system makes her do it."

"Bill, are you determined to embarrass me?"

"Somebody has to embarrass you, my dear. Otherwise, you'll look like meee before you're my age. You're making a fortune being an innocent. So beeee one! As long as you caaaan."

"Bill!"

He bowed slightly to Mrs. Roosevelt. "You'll forgive me, I hope. I'm just doing my missionary worrrrk. I'm an agent of saaalvation, y'understaaand."

"I quite understand, Mr. Fields," said the First Lady. "Saving by precept if not by example."

Fields laughed heartily. "Tooooou-ché,

gracious lady! Well spoke! Well spoke, in-deeeed."

Fred Allen hurried up. "We can start the auction now, so as not to take too much of your time," he said.

"I have set aside the evening for this affair, Mr. Allen."

"Then let me introduce you around a bit. Bill. Judy. Thank you. Mrs. Roosevelt will see you again later."

She had met some of the celebrities before. Bud Abbot and Lou Costello had been to the White House during a previous war bond drive. Costello was still as she remembered him: a little unsure as to how an actor who played his particular broad-comic character should behave in the presence of the First Lady. Jack Benny vividly remembered the days they had spent together on the *Normandie* during the crossing in 1938. She had not met Laurel and Hardy before and found them modest, genial men, a pleasure to talk to. And Wallace Beery, for all the rough-hewn characters he played, was a soft-spoken man with a ready smile, deferential to the First Lady and restrained in conversation.

Fred Allen opened the auction. His nasal voice made him an amusing auctioneer. In the course of two hours he sold $34,250 worth of war bonds. He announced the standing offer by Hedy Lamarr to give "a great big kiss" to any man who bought $25,000 worth of war bonds, but there were no takers.

Mrs. Roosevelt was pleased that her autographed picture brought a high bid of $1,200.

V

"Wednesday? Wednesday, and you hadn't told me?"

Mrs. Roosevelt shrugged. "What could you have done about it, Franklin? You have burdens to carry. If I can relieve you of this one . . ."

"At it again, old girl," he said, shaking his head, yet conceding a smile.

The President passed a bit of toast to Fala, and the little black dog chewed vigorously.

As she did most mornings, the First Lady had come to the President's bedroom as he finished his breakfast. He sat propped up against half a dozen pillows, tray across his lap, the bed littered with the newspapers he had been scanning when she entered. She had come carrying, as usual, a small list of things she wanted to discuss with him.

"Are you aware of the situation in Bridgeport, Connecticut?" she asked.

"What situation is that?" the President asked, breaking off another bite of toast for Fala.

"It is being suggested," she told him, "that the employment service will not refer Negro women to jobs in war plants, where they could earn far more than they earn as domestic servants, because the area housewives do not want to lose their servants."

"Is there any truth to it?"

"I don't know. I'd like to find out. There is a rumor also that Negro women appear at war plants carrying slips of paper that say, 'Please give this woman a job. E.R.' Of course, I have never signed such a note. But—"

"I'll inquire of the War Manpower Commission," said the President. "Next. What else do you want to worry me with— omitting murder in the White House, in my map room in fact? What else?"

In her study a few minutes later, the First Lady received a telephone call from the Department of the Navy—

"Mrs. Roosevelt? This is Captain David Bloom of Naval Intelligence, Cryptanalysis Division. I wonder if you could give me half an hour to review with you the analysis we have done of the letters you gave to Secretary Knox?"

"Certainly, Captain. How soon can you be here?"

He could be there in half an hour, and was—a brisk, bustling, efficient man, carrying a strapped-shut leather briefcase. He carried his white cap correctly under his arm. His compact head was shiny bald. His hazel eyes, under black brows, were so small and intense that some would have called them beady.

In Mrs. Roosevelt's study he sat down and opened his briefcase. He extracted a sheaf of papers.

"To be altogether frank with you, Ma'am," he said, "if it were anyone but you, I would decline to discuss this subject at all."

"I quite understand," she said.

He glanced around the room. Maybe the sight of her family pictures and of her favorite ship model eased his tension a little. In any event, he abandoned a bit of his stiffness.

"The letters you sent to Secretary Knox have been thoroughly examined," he said. "One of them is a coded message. The other is not, so far as we can determine."

"I wondered . . ."

"The letter ostensibly signed by a Miss Chin Yu-lin is not in any code of which we are aware. It is of course possible that it is coded—in a private code between the sender and the recipient, that only they could understand. Such codes are not uncommon, as between two specific people. No one but those two people can possibly read the code."

"I think I understand."

"Well, for example— I might agree with you that if in a letter I refer to Tuesday in any context, that is a report that a certain event has taken place, whereas if I mention Wednesday it means the event has not taken place. Only you and I know that. Only you and I know what event I am talking about. There are a number of references in the Chin Yu-lin letter that could be of that nature."

"But we can't be sure?"

"There is no way we can be sure."

"Then we come to the 'Ben' letter."

"Yes. Far more interesting. It is written in a Japanese cipher: a code we have intercepted, analyzed, and deciphered. We haven't seen it for some time. It used to be common. It was used, for example, by Japanese agents advising the Japanese navy of the precise location of specific ships in Pearl Harbor."

"They did that? Then—"

"Then we should have known they were going to attack Pearl Harbor? I wish our intelligence problems had been that simple. Reports in the same code located ships in Manila harbor, Hong Kong, Singapore . . . Also airplanes on various fields throughout the Pacific. Army units. And so on. In any event, it was a spy code. We've seen very few examples of it since December 1941."

"Is it a terribly difficult code?" Mrs. Roosevelt asked.

"It was until we broke it, late in 1939. It has some highly sophisticated elements. Look at this paragraph—"

He pointed to the paragraph in the letter that read—

> You'll remember at the sales meeting Doug put a lot of emphasis on 23-1424 and 23-1543. It turns out those items aren't selling so hot out here, so I'd work more on old standbys like 17-6555 and 17-7654. Men like the tried and true, I guess. On the ladies styles though you should push items like 23-3432 and 23-3433. Personally I couldn't believe the gals would go for those heels, but I guess something like that has special appeal in drab times.

"It doesn't take much smarts to suspect that those numbers, supposedly shoe-model numbers, mean something else entirely. Also, if you intercept a lot of traffic, you can begin to attach meaning to the code numbers. For example, in the spring of 1942 we were intercepting Japanese naval radio traffic that mentioned 'AF.' Obviously, something was going to happen at or near AF. But what and where was AF? Well, in March, a couple of Japanese seaplanes refueled from a subma-

rine. They rendezvoused with that submarine at French Frigate Shoals. This we
knew. In one of their radio reports, the
seaplanes mentioned flying near AF. The
only thing of any consequence between
their home base and French Frigate Shoals
was Midway. So . . . AF was Midway. As
the weeks went by, we began to see more
and more references to AF. That meant
something big was about to happen at
Midway. So we prepared for it. And well
we did."

"So you know what these numbers
mean—like 23-1424 and 23-1453, and so
on."

"We do. But there is more to it than
that. Those numbers can have various
meanings. There is not just one key to the
code. There are several. Something else in
the letter tells the spy which key to use."

"Ah. And what is that?"

"Look at the sentence telling the
'salesman' what cities to visit. You notice,
he says, 'I figure you can get in a good
three or four weeks working Wash., Philly,
NY, Boston & Baltimore and still get back
to SF in plenty of time for your wedding.'

Does it seem to you that is an odd way to list those cities?"

"Well, I suppose so. I think I might mention them north to south or vice versa."

"Do you see what order they are in?" asked Captain Bloom, faintly smiling. He enjoyed puzzles and would be interested to see if the First Lady could solve this one. "Do you see?"

Mrs. Roosevelt nodded. "Reverse alphabetical order," she said.

"Exactly," said Captain Bloom, his smile widening. "The way those cities are listed told us this very likely was a coded message. It also suggested what code was used. Messages using this code always include a list of names—people, cities . . . whatever. Things listed are always in alphabetical order, reverse alphabetical order, or at random, no order at all. There are three keys to the code. The order of the list tells the spy which key to use."

"Then these numbers . . ."

"Yes. You ignore the numbers to the left of the hyphen. They are meaningless. Also, since the list is in reverse alphabetical order, the numbers must be reversed.

So, 23-1424 is 4241. 23-1543 is 3451. And so on."

"I see."

"Intercepted messages contain more than five hundred such numbers. We know what maybe twenty percent of them mean. Fortunately, we know more about which ones refer to geographical places than which ones refer to ships or military units."

"Then, what is your judgment, Captain, about the meaning of the 'Ben' letter?"

Captain Bloom frowned and nodded. "It may be fanciful to suppose that 'Doug' refers to General MacArthur. Probably it *is* fanciful. On the other hand, 'Doug' may be a general reference to the United States or to the Allied command in the South Pacific. In any case, we know that 4241 means Rabaul. We think 3451 means Hollandia. We're not sure. It seems very likely, then, that the first sentence of the paragraph means that Japan thinks the United States plans to attack Rabaul and maybe Hollandia. If you look at a map of the South Pacific, you will see this is logical."

Mrs. Roosevelt did not have to go to the Map Room to visualize this. Opening a drawer in her desk, she took out a *National Geographic* map of the South Pacific. The big Japanese naval base at Rabaul was some six hundred miles west of Gaudalcanal. The Japanese base at Hollandia, New Guinea, was some fourteen hundred miles from Guadalcanal. A drive to recapture the Philippines could not succeed until Rabaul was reduced. Hollandia was an essential step on the road to Manila.

Captain Bloom went on—" 'I'd work more on old standbys like 17-6555 and 17-7654.' We know that 5556 is Ceylon. We're not at all sure what 4567 is. It could be the Maldives. Anyway, the message seems to be telling the spy to concentrate on Ceylon, plus maybe the Maldive Islands. Ceylon would be key to an invasion of India. The Japs have raided it more than once."

"Fascinating," murmured Mrs. Roosevelt.

"The letter goes on to say the spy should 'push' items like 2343 and 3343. Those are numbers that come up from time to time in this code. We are not sure, but we think they refer to naval concentrations and aircraft concentrations."

"In other words," said the First Lady, "the spy was being instructed to find out what he could about naval and air forces on Ceylon and in the Maldive Islands."

Captain Bloom nodded. "You must understand, though, that we could be altogether wrong. They can have changed their codes. Other factors can be wrong. Our brilliant crew at Pearl Harbor guessed right, from no more information than this, about the attack on Midway. Other times, we have been one hundred percent off."

The First Lady picked up her telephone. "Captain," she said, "would you care for a cup of tea? Or coffee? With a bite of fruit or a cinnamon bun?"

The captain stiffened, as if surprised. "How very kind," he said. "I would appreciate a cup of coffee and a cinnamon bun."

Mrs. Roosevelt gave the order to the pantry.

"Of one thing you are sure," she continued. "You are sure this letter *is* a coded letter, using a Japanese espionage code."

"Ma'am . . . The chances of such

numbers occurring together in a letter that is not a spy message are—"

"Infinitesimal," she said, seeing that he was searching for a word.

"Infinitesimal," he agreed.

"You will of course give this information to Admiral King."

"I have already put the information into channels," he said. "I said the coded letter came from an 'impeccable source.' I did not say it came from you."

"Do you think the letter means the Japanese are planning an invasion of Ceylon?"

"We can't be sure. The letter offers a suggestion. It justifies an alert in the Indian Ocean. Increased air reconnaissance. That sort of thing. More information will be needed before significant forces are committed."

"Would the information seem more momentous if it were known where it came from?" she asked.

"I'm sure it would, Ma'am."

"Then we must let Admiral King know where it came from. I will take care of that."

* * *

Saturday noon was the occasion for a luncheon for Madame Chiang Kai-shek and some American publishers. Once again, the President had refused, unconditionally—no matter that it might annoy Madame Chiang—to invite Henry ("Loose with the Truth") Luce to the White House, any more than he would have invited Bertie ("Dirty Bertie Hitler-flirty") McCormick. The publishers of *Time* and the *Chicago Tribune* had exceeded even Franklin Roosevelt's elastic tolerance about journalistic ethics.

In fact, the President had limited the press luncheon to the "working stiffs" who covered the White House day in and day out—whom, he judged, deserved a chance to beard the Dragon Lady and write scoops.

Beard her they did—

—"Madame Chiang, exactly how many divisions can the Generalissimo put in the field? With increased American aid? Without it?"

—"We have been told, Madame, that your niece is a direct lineal descendant of Confucius. Is she a Christian also, as you are?"

—"Please comment, Madame Chiang,

about the relationship between the Generalissimo and Mr. Mao Tse-tung and Mr. Chou En-lai. And, specifically, does the Generalissimo regard the Japanese or Mr. Mao as his principal enemy?"

— "What, exactly, is the meaning of the term *generalissimo?* Who else uses it as a title?"

— "In postwar China, assuming we win, will Generalissimo Chiang Kai-shek submit his government and its record to a free and open general election?"

The President did not intervene. He sat with his cigarette atilt and listened to Madame Chiang field the questions, a little too conspicuously amused, in Mrs. Roosevelt's judgment.

Madame Chiang fielded them well. She did not field them well. What you thought depended on your judgment of her, of her husband, of China . . .

She laughed some questions off. She replied to others with clichés and epigrams.

Responding to the question of which was the principal enemy, the Chinese Communists or the Japanese, she said, "When one faces a leopard and a panther, one does not weigh them as more dangerous or less dangerous. One defends first against the one that attacks first and hopes to survive to defend against the other."

The meaning of the word *generalissimo*—"Poor China has more generals than it can afford. My husband would call himself 'lieutenant' if the country were only full of sergeants."

Elections—"It is easy to hold an election in the United States, where one government controls all the people and territory. How can we hold an election in China before we restore unity?"

Mrs. Nesbitt had prepared trays of tuna-fish sandwiches for this luncheon. When the reporters left and Madame Chiang returned to the Queen's Suite, Mrs. Roosevelt noticed that only a few of the sandwiches had been eaten. She suggested to the people carrying them back to the kitchen that they become the day's lunch for the White House staff.

"It won't work, you know," said Elinor Morgenthau, her personal friend of many years, wife of the Secretary of the Treasury—a petite, attractive, dark-haired woman.

"What won't work, Elinor?"

"In the short run. The small problem. Those inedible damned sandwiches will be scraped into the garbage can. The bigger problem is what the newspapers will publish."

"Meaning?"

"The working newspapermen who just confronted the Dragon Lady will write stories saying what she is and what she said. And their publishers will not publish them. To the publishers, she's a heroine—a slant-eyed, slit-skirted Joan of Arc. Because she's a good Methodist."

"Elinor . . ."

"Have you seen what the *Chicago Intelligencer* has done to you today?"

"Something new? Something different?"

"Better read it," said Elinor Morgenthau, handing over a newspaper. Even Bertie McCormick might have been a little more restrained."

Editorial. *Chicago Intelligencer*—

Last evening the redoubtable Eleanor Roosevelt attended a so-called "Bond Rally" in Washington, at which innocents were encouraged to bid, in terms of war bond purchases, for an assortment of worthless junk donated by publicity-grabbing celebrities—including La Eleanor herself, who donated (how could we resist?) an autographed photograph of herself hobnobbing with England's tinpot royalty.

At the very same hour in New York an obese and frowzy woman called Sophie Tucker ("Last of the Red-Hot Mamas") conducted a similar auction, at which "patriots" could bid on such values as a G-string worn by Gypsy Rose Lee, a pair of net opera stockings worn by Margie Hart, a pair of "pasties" once glued to the bosoms of Anne Corio, and a pair of feathered fans once used by Sally Rand.

We are not finished. In Hollywood, a few months ago, a group of "starlets"—one Lucille Ball, one Veronica Lake, one Anne Sheridan, and one Donna Reed—haven't-beens and never-will-be's—played a game of "strip poker" for newsreel cameras, the frilly clothing the young ladies shed to go to "relief" for Londoners whose clothes were burned in German incendiary raids. Happily, the complaisant girls stopped their game when they were down to their unmentionables. One wonders how the women of London's East End will receive the silken skirts and blouses the "starlets" shed.

Surely our country can carry its burden in this war without such foolish and immoral shenanigans. That the wife of the President should lend her presence and name to such spectacles is but another episode in the shameful career of Eleanor Roosevelt.

Let the President rein in La Eleanor. She has long been an embarrassment to him and to the American people. Is there to be no end? Shame! Shame! Shame that our boys fighting overseas should have to hide their faces because their "First Lady" makes herself party to whatever her "crowd" contrives. We know who her "crowd" are. Can't we, even in wartime, put down her assorted nuts, radicals, and traitors?

Mrs. Roosevelt handed the newspaper back to Elinor Morgenthau. "Bit much, isn't it?" she said quietly.

"They think they can't hurt you," said Elinor Morgenthau.

"No. They think they can. They mean to. Little people. They can't win votes, so they resort to vicious attacks on those who can. The American people have rejected them. In their frustration, they lash out—angry, hysterical . . . Despicable."

Elinor Morgenthau frowned. She had never before heard her friend talk this way. She had supposed attacks couldn't hurt Eleanor. Now she knew they could.

The tall, spare, sepulchral Chief of Naval Operations met with Mrs. Roosevelt in the Map Room. Admiral Ernest King was a formidable man: competent, efficient, demanding.

"I am responsible for your not having been told until now just where the coded letter came from," said Mrs. Roosevelt. "I handed the letters to Secretary Knox, who in turn handed them to the cryptanalysts."

"The information may be worthless, or it may be very important," said Admiral King. "To evaluate it, we needed to know where it came from."

"As you can readily imagine," said Mrs. Roosevelt, "the fact that there has been a murder in the White House—and not only in the White House but on the second floor and during the visit of Madame Chiang Kai-shek—is a grave matter that we have been trying to keep entirely confidential."

"Naval Intelligence," said the admiral dryly, "has some little experience with keeping secrets."

"As have I, Admiral King."

The suggestion of a smile flickered across the admiral's impassive face. "The Japanese," he said, "mounted a major offensive toward Midway last year. If we had lost Midway, Hawaii would have been in grave danger. But we checked that offensive. Their campaign in the Solomon Islands was, of course, the first stage in an offensive against Australia. We checked that at Guadalcanal. We have to suppose they will try somewhere else. They raided Ceylon last year. Maybe that was a reconnaissance. If they took Ceylon and established air and naval bases on the island, they would threaten India from two sides. Actually, the Maldives might suit their purposes better. There, they could establish powerful bases and wouldn't have to hold down much in the way of a hostile local population. I think we have to take this spy letter very seriously."

The First Lady nodded thoughtfully and glanced around the Map Room. "It is difficult to understand why the man would have entered this room," she said. "He could learn nothing here. Nothing on the maps in this room indicates the disposition of our forces or anything about plans."

"Maybe he was in the wrong room," said Admiral King.

"But why?"

"Have you considered the possibility that maybe this room was not his objective at all, that maybe what he wanted to do was go from here into the President's study and from there into the President's bedroom?"

"Both doors are strong and securely locked."

"Well . . . He got in *here.*"

"I'd rather not even think of the possibility," she said. "What is worse, at least two more people got in—and killed the man."

Admiral King rose from his chair and went to squint at a map. It showed the Indian Ocean and the Bay of Bengal, with adjoining lands. For a moment he stood and stared, and Mrs. Roosevelt guessed he was looking at Ceylon and the Maldive Islands, pondering, perhaps, where he might find the naval strength to blunt a Japanese attack on them.

"I know I shouldn't ask," she said, "but will this letter require you to divert forces from some other theater of operations to reinforce our forces in the Indian Ocean?"

" 'Reinforce' is not the word," said Admiral King. "We *have* no forces in the Indian Ocean."

"Oh, dear!"

"It's no secret. The Japanese know it well."

"I dislike thinking of a major movement of forces based on no better evidence than this letter," she said.

"It can't be major. We haven't major forces to spare."

"Even so—"

"This letter may be a godsend. Or it may not. In any case, I am glad to have it. I will keep your secret—as I know you will keep mine."

The President went to bed early that Saturday evening, and Mrs. Roosevelt alone took dinner with Madame Chiang. Elinor Morgenthau was the First Lady's guest. Mr. and Miss Kung and the venerable Weng Guo-fang were Madame Chiang's. They ate in the private dining room.

To her surprise, Mrs. Roosevelt learned that Madame Chiang had sent down an order for pheasant and wild rice, with iced champagne. Mrs. Nesbitt called for advice, and the First Lady told her to meet the Madame's order if she could. Also, a serving should be sent to the President on his dinner tray. The macaroni-and-cheese casserole could be saved for tomorrow.

Weng Guo-fang talked about China—

"It was not wrong, in my belief, for our people to believe, as they did for many centuries, that our country was the Middle Kingdom, the center of the world, to call our country the Celestial Empire, to refer to the Emperor as Son of Heaven. All was very beautiful, once. Only shadows remain, and even they are enough to show us what once was, what must once have been."

"Mr. Weng served the Empress Dowager," said Madame Chiang.

"They say she was very beautiful," said Mrs. Roosevelt.

"She was," he said, with an elegantly respectful tone even in his reminiscence. "She had been, you know, a concubine. It was only through great beauty, exceptional intelligence, and practiced skill that she became what she was. She was also capable of extreme cruelty."

"Of which many suffered," said Miss Kung.

"She was last of the Manchus," said Weng Guo-fang sadly. "I think she would have died rather than abdicate. Henry Pu Yi is—" The old man shook his head curtly, and Mrs. Roosevelt guessed if he had been out of doors he would have spat. "He is a despicable little man. The last Emperor? No. *She* was the last."

Elinor Morgenthau shifted her eyes to Madame Chiang. "Perhaps a new dynasty may be founded," she said.

Madame Chiang Kai-shek nodded. "Perhaps . . . someday," she said quietly.

VI

When Captain Ed Kennelly and Agent Robert Kirkwal arrived in the President's oval study about nine o'clock on Sunday morning, they found the President seated in his wheelchair, staring glumly at the First Lady's crayon-scribbled chart of KNOWNs and UNKNOWNs—

KNOWN

1. Death occurred between 8:12 and 8:57 P.M.
2. At least two persons were involved.
3. Victim was inebriated.
4. Victim was known as George Shen since at least September 1942, when he got a driver's license.
5. Map Room lock was picked.
6. No one yet identified saw Shen in WH. (But <u>someone</u> saw him.)
7. Map Room not specifically guarded.

UNKNOWN

1. ~~Identity and business of Shen.~~
2. ~~His reason for being in WH.~~
3. Who killed him?
4. Why?
5. How did Shen enter WH?

"We know who he was and why he was here," she said, explaining why she had run thick lines through two of her unknowns.

The President looked up. Good morning, Bobby," he said to Kirkwal. "Good to see you, too, Ed—though I could wish we met on happier occasions."

A breakfast buffet had already been set up on a table, and the President had already filled his plate with ham and eggs, plus buttered toast. Mrs. Roosevelt poured him a cup of coffee.

"Serve yourselves, gentlemen," said the President. "Don't be bashful. Fill your plates. We have things to talk about, and you are going to need your strength."

Besides ham and eggs and bacon and toast, the buffet also featured sliced melon, grapes, and apples, cinnamon buns and sugar Danish, coffee and tea.

"Look at what someone has sent me," said the President, reaching to his desk and picking up a photograph. "What on earth do you suppose that is meant to be?"

The picture was of a bicycle handlebars and saddle, welded together.

"That," said the President, "is the head of a bull—according to Monsieur Pablo Picasso."

Ed Kennelly frowned over the picture. "Looks like a pair of handlebars and a bicycle seat to me," he said.

Mrs. Roosevelt smiled on this exchange. The President had shown her the picture earlier and had enjoyed his little essay at wit. To her, the interesting part of the picture was that Picasso had done the small sculpture in occupied Paris. The Germans had allowed photos of the work to go out through Switzerland.

"Something else interesting," said the President. "I've been reading in the papers about a Frenchman called Cousteau who's invented a contraption that lets him swim around under the water for as long as he wants to. It's not a diving suit with air hoses coming down. He carries his air in a tank on his back. Now, imagine that. I'd think the fish are going to be awfully annoyed. They won't have a bit of privacy left."

While they ate, the President commented on other items in the news—a new German offensive in Russia, for one, and the defeat of Rommel in Tunisia. When all of them had finished eating and were only sipping coffee, he turned to the matter of the murder in the Map Room.

"You fellows are into something that's got major war-plans implications," he said. "We're faced with two alternatives, as I see it. Either I trust you with what may be a major military secret, or we take you off the case and turn the murder investigation over to John Edgar Hoover."

"Whichever you choose, Mr. President," said Kirkwal.

"Ed?"

"Whichever way you want it," said Kennelly.

"I'd like to have you stay on the job," said the President. "The problem is, you'll have to have security clearances. The problem is, in order to get you those security clearances, we'll have to induct you into the armed forces."

Kennelly chuckled. "Seaman First Class Edward Kennelly reporting for duty, Sir. In the last war. Served on a destroyer."

"Bobby?"

"I've never served in the forces, Sir. I'm a naturalized citizen. I'd just became nineteen when they stopped drafting."

"Well, unless you strenuously object, you are now Commander Robert Kirkwal, USNR. And Ed, that's a big jump for you— from seaman first class to commander."

"I used to say I'd refuse to be made an officer," said Kennelly. "But— It will be quite an honor, Mr. President."

"You won't even need uniforms," said the President. He grinned. "Of course, you can buy them if you want them. You are assigned to detached duty, directly under the Secretary of the Navy. You can continue to do exactly what you are doing— including being a captain of the District police, Ed. In fact, you don't even need to tell anyone you are naval officers."

Kennelly grinned. "I can think of one or two I'm going to tell."

The President laughed, then turned somber. "Both of you understand why you are being inducted and commissioned. Very simply, if you should disclose anything of what you learn in the course of this investigation, you can be court-martialed and shot. You are under orders from this moment on not to disclose a single word of what we now think is involved in the murder in the Map Room—not that I ever entertained the slightest suspicion you would. But to solve this crime you may need some information that comes from intelligence sources. We could not give you that information without inducting you."

"In other words," said Kennelly, "our man George Shen was a spy."

The President nodded. "The Missus will explain more fully. But it looks like we may have to move a small naval task force to counter what's suggested in the coded letter found on Shen. The Nips undoubtedly know by now that their man Shen is dead. What they don't know is that he was carrying a coded letter—and, of course, they have no idea that we've cracked their code and can read what appears to have been Shen's instructions."

Kirkwal was looking at Mrs. Roosevelt's chart. "The question of how the man got into the White House is what troubles me most," he said. "Our security is really very good."

"I'm at least as concerned about how his murderers got in," said the President. "I'd like to think I'm safe here."

"Maybe the murderers didn't get in," said Kennelly. "Maybe they were already inside the White House."

The President raised his chin high, and his eyes narrowed. "You're thinking about the Dragon Lady's staff?"

"Well . . . Suppose the Chinese saw Shen and recognized him for a Jap spy. Is it crazy to think they might just do him in?"

"Summary execution," said Mrs. Roosevelt.

"Madame Chiang has a male secretary and an errand boy—the young man we've called the factotum—on her staff," said Kirkwal. "We've surmised that pair are bodyguards."

"Can anyone attach names to them?" the President asked.

"Yes, Sir," said Kirkwal. "The secretary is T'sa Yuang-hung. The factotum is Liang P'ing."

"Write those names down for me," said the President. "I'll get off a message to General Stilwell, see if he knows anything about that pair."

"Their whereabouts is not accounted for at the time of the murder," said Kirkwal. "Which is only to say that they were apparently in the rooms assigned them on the third floor."

"I assume you haven't interrogated them."

"We haven't interrogated any of Madame Chiang's staff."

"I think you're going to have to find out more about the dead man. I'm glad we know he was a spy, but that fact alone doesn't explain why somebody killed him."

"Why somebody killed him *in the White House,*" said Mrs. Roosevelt.

The President glanced at his watch. "Well," he said. "I have to go to work— believe it or not—Sunday though it may be. You fellows have your work cut out for you. Beware of the Missus here. She loves her Sherlock Holmes persona—loves it rather too much, I've sometimes thought."

"We are grateful for her help, Mr. President," said Kirkwal.

"So am I, Bobby. So am I."

Madame Chiang Kai-shek attended church services. Mrs. Roosevelt accompanied her. The First Lady suggested they simply walk across Lafayette Park to St. John's, but Madame Chiang said she would prefer to go by car. So they arrived at the church in a black limousine preceded by motorcycles with sirens. The Madame waved happily at the assembled newspaper photographers who took pictures of her as she went in and came out. Mrs. Roosevelt was reminded of a comment she'd heard one Sunday morning from the mouth of Representative Everett Dirksen of Illinois, who said, "Not much point in coming to church, is there, if nobody takes notice?"

Returning briefly—as he thought—to police headquarters, Ed Kennelly found a message waiting for him. He'd sent officers around to hotels and rooming houses, carrying a photograph of the late George Shen. One of them had found out where the man had stayed.

Kennelly phoned Kirkwal. "You want to go with me while I take a look at the room?"

Kirkwal wanted to go. Half an hour later they pulled up in front of a big old white frame house on Thirteenth Street. A small sign affixed to the porch railing read—

ROOM AND BOARD
RESPECTABLE ONLY

"It's a Negro neighborhood," said Kennelly. "And 'respectable' is the word. These are the old-time Washington Negroes, descendants of the slaves that lived here before the Civil War."

"As distinguished from what?" Kirkwal asked.

"Well . . . as distinguished from the Negroes who came up from the South during the worst years of the Depression. I mean, the people who live around here own their homes and take a lot of pride in that. Most of the more recent Negroes can't own homes yet."

"Why do you suppose our Chinese friend chose to take room and board here?"

"Could be a lot of reasons. It made him hard to locate. But I've got an idea he rented here because it was the only place he could find. You know how it is, trying to find a place to live in Washington these days."

Kennelly turned the key in the doorbell on the door, and the big gong inside rang authoritatively.

A handsome, dark woman, in her forties, likely, came to the door. She confronted the two men with a skeptical eye, a raised chin. "Gen'men . . . ?"

Kennelly showed his badge. "Captain Ed Kennelly, District police," he said. "And this is Commander Robert Kirkwal, Naval Intelligence. We would like to inquire about a roomer of yours."

The woman stepped back from the door. "I am Mrs. Thaddeus Forsythe," she said. "I own and manage this house. You may come in."

They walked into the late nineteenth century. The entrance hall floor was covered with linoleum in a blue-and-white pattern of blossoms and leaves, gleaming with wax. Potted palms flourished in tubs to either side of the wide walnut staircase. The walls were papered with floral wallpaper, much of it covered by the dozen or so big, framed family portraits—sepia-toned photographs—that stared down on the hallway with a vague air of disapproval.

Mrs. Forsythe beckoned them to follow her into her parlor. There, too, the nineteenth century prevailed: a clutter of knickknacks, horsehair-upholstered furniture, more portraits, vases of dried flowers, a piano, and in the corner, a formidable cello.

"You have a problem with one of my tenants?" she asked, pointing toward the chairs where they might sit.

"Do you rent a room to a Mr. George Shen, a Chinese man?"

"Well, maybe I do and maybe I don't," she said. "Yes, Mr. Shen rented a room and was here about a week, but then he disappeared. His rent will become due on Wednesday, and if he does not appear to renew, I will put his things in a storage room and give his room to someone else."

"We would like to see his room," said Kennelly.

"I suppose technically I should ask if you have a warrant."

"I can promise you Mr. Shen won't object to our seeing his room," said Kennelly. "He's dead."

Mrs. Forsythe gasped, then quickly recovered her composure.

"I suppose you are going to tell me he's been murdered," she said. "I suppose you are going to tell me he was really Japanese and a spy."

"Interesting guesses," said Kennelly.

She shrugged. "Why else would a D.C. police captain and an officer of Naval Intelligence come and inquire about him?"

"Tell us what you know about Shen," said Kennelly.

"He came here on Wednesday, February 10. He said he needed a room for about two weeks and a cab driver had told him I had a vacancy. As it happened, I *had* a vacancy, though it's unusual for any rooming house to have one these days."

"Did he eat at your table?"

"Two nights. That's all. Some of my longtime tenants felt he did not want to eat with Negroes. He was the only— Well, what would you call him? All the rest of my tenants are Negroes."

"Did he tell you what was his occupation?" Kirkwal asked.

"He said he sold shoes for a living. Wholesale. Represented a manufacturer. I noticed he didn't have a sample case."

"Did he talk at dinner?"

"Not much. Listened mostly. Said the war was hard on his business. Shoe rationing, you know."

"So . . . Can we see his room?"

Mrs. Forsythe nodded and led the two men to the second floor.

George Shen had rented what was very likely the smallest room in the house: a small, square bedroom at the rear, overlooking an alley, without toilet or basin. It was a room, Mrs. Forsythe explained, usually occupied by men who took it in the hope they would graduate to one of the bigger rooms sooner or later.

It was, on the other hand, neat and clean. The bed was made. Shen's bags were laid out on luggage stands. His clothes hung in a big old-fashioned wardrobe.

"I make and change the beds," said Mrs. Forsythe. "When I do, I hang up things or fold them into drawers. If a man needs too much of that kind of service, I ask him to leave."

"You rent only to men?" asked Kirkwal.

"Well, it's got to be one or the other," she said. "Men or women. Contrary to what people suppose, it's the men who are neatest, cleanest."

"I'm sorry, Mrs. Forsythe," said Kennelly, "but we've got to go through his things. You can stay and watch if you want. Or—"

"I'll leave," she said. "Police business. I didn't know the man well enough to mourn. I—"

"You will understand," said Kirkwal, "that the death of Mr. Shen is—or, at least, may be—a matter involving military secrets. Your two guesses may or may not have been correct. We would appreciate it, in any case, if you—"

"Kept my mouth shut."

Kennelly grinned. "Well said."

What Shen had left behind vividly told the two investigators that he had meant to return to this room, had never dreamed he would not. In a small leather case in the inside jacket pocket of his spare suit he had carried two photographs of a young woman, presumably the Chin Yu-lin who had written him about their impending marriage. She was an exquisitely beautiful girl—no older than twenty-one, the two men judged from her pictures. In one she wore a flower-patterned dress and a tiny straw hat with veil. In the other she was stark naked.

"I suggest we don't show this to Mrs. Roosevelt," said Kennelly, pointing at the nude.

Kirkwal shrugged. "I have no strong opinion."

The labels in the clothes suggested nothing but San Francisco. But—

"They don't look to me like the wardrobe of a wholesale shoe salesman," said Kennelly.

"The wardrobe of a Japanese-language interpreter for O and O Steamships," said Kirkwal.

"Possibly."

"Here's the most interesting thing," said Kirkwal.

It was a map. Folded and refolded to the point that the fold lines were breaking, stained and smudged, it was a Japanese military map, printed on paper backed with silk. Not a *National Geographic* map, this one was made to be carried by an officer in combat, designed to get wet without disintegrating.

The area covered was the ocean west of the Dutch East Indies—the Strait of Malacca, the Bay of Bengal, the Indian Ocean, Ceylon, the Maldive Islands, and the coasts of India. Columns of tiny Japanese characters adjacent to bays and harbors probably indicated the kinds of shipping that could enter.

"Interesting," Kennelly agreed.

For his part, he picked up other things and stuffed them in envelopes: a toothbrush, a razor, a pencil, a fingernail clipper . . . a Bible lying on the nightstand, which might be Mrs. Forsythe's. So, he could return it to her later—if this particular Bible did not contain a key to some devilish code. He wrapped it in a sheet of newspaper. He took a bottle of aspirin tablets—which might not be aspirin—for lab analysis.

Kirkwal had unfolded the map and spread it on the bed. A small, square sheet of paper had been folded inside. It was nearly transparent paper, maybe cut from a sheet of onionskin. A group of numbers were written on it in ink.

"This may be damned important," said Kirkwal. "Wasn't one of the numbers in the 'Ben' letter 5566? I don't remember what 5566 was supposed to stand for, but I think it was one of the numbers. Look at the way these numbers are written—not in a column but scattered over the paper. I bet you that when you lay this sheet on the map and put 5566 on whatever it is, the other numbers are the codes for other places."

"Mrs. Roosevelt will definitely want to see that," said Kennelly.

"Maybe even the President will want to see it," said Kirkwal.

Captain David Bloom, the Navy cryptanalyst, arrived at the White House a little after five, protesting that it was no inconvenience at all to be asked to come on Sunday afternoon. He was glad to do it, hoped he could be of service.

They met in the Map Room—the President and Mrs. Roosevelt, Kennelly and Kirkwal, and Captain Bloom.

"We know that 5556 is Ceylon," said Bloom. "So . . . Suppose we lay this bit of paper over the map so 5556 is on Ceylon. Aha! We line up the bottom of the paper on the Equator . . . the left edge along the line of seventy degrees east longitude. And so!"

"So?" asked the President?

"Well, 4567 turns out to be the Maldives, as we guessed. And 1231 is the Port of Madras, 2865 is the Andaman Islands, 3567 is Rangoon. And so on."

"I wonder," said the President, "what this man's spymasters would have thought if they had known he had written down his map key and folded it into his map."

"I expect they would have shot him," said Captain Bloom.

"Not a very adept spy," said the President. "Rather clumsy, in fact."

"He got into the White House," said Mrs. Roosevelt.

"And got himself killed here," said the President.

"This information," said Bloom, tapping the map and the onionskin with one finger, "is very useful. We've guessed at the meaning of these numbers but were never really sure of most of them. Just look at the possibilities here! A Japanese fleet based in the Maldive Islands could render the Suez Canal virtually worthless to the British. It could block shipping coming out of the Gulf of Aden. It could savage the west-coast ports of India, like Bombay."

"To stop them," said the President, "we would have to send a fleet of our own into the Indian Ocean. And we hardly have the ships to spare for that. We have a two-ocean navy, not a three-ocean navy."

Captain Bloom refolded the Japanese map. "I am afraid I have additional discouraging news, Mr. President," he said. "These numbers—I mean the numbers on the sheet of onionskin—have been coming up in our intercepts of Japanese naval radio traffic. Not often. Occasionally. But a lot more often than ever before."

The President shook his head. "I don't

know where the ships are going to come from."

When the others left, the First Lady walked beside the President as he wheeled himself into the West Sitting Hall. He found General Edwin "Pa" Watson, Admiral Ross McIntyre, his doctor and Harry Hopkins waiting to share his cocktail hour.

Before she left him to walk on into her study, Mrs. Roosevelt put a hand on his shoulder. "Try to relax," she said softly. "You look tired and tense."

He looked up. "On top of everything else," he said, "I'm being deviled by John L. Lewis. He's talking about taking his miners out on strike. In the middle of the war! Can you imagine?"

"He thinks of nothing but the men he represents," she said.

"Yes. He said the other day that the country would be better off without Franklin D. Roosevelt in the White House. Tell you what. I'll make him a deal. I'll resign the presidency if he'll commit suicide."

She smiled. "I shall probably be see-

ing him tomorrow. Shall I put that propo-
sition to him?"

"I wish you would."

Madame Chiang Kai-shek left the
White House for the evening, to dine with
her friend Henry Luce. She went alone, accompanied only by the secretary T'sa
Yuang-hung, who looked more and more
like a bodyguard.

Mrs. Roosevelt went out, too. She
dined with a small committee of women
from the A.F. of L. and the C.I.O., who
wanted to convey to the President their
special concern about inflation, which they
said was impoverishing American workers
in spite of wartime price controls.

The First Lady promised to tell the
President how deeply concerned they
were.

She returned to the White House a little after ten. A telephone message slip on
her desk said she should call Edward
Greschner, publisher of the *San Francisco
Chronicle,* at home. The White House operator put the call through, and in a few
minutes she was talking to Greschner.

"Interesting development," he said. "Miss Chin Yu-lin went into police headquarters this morning and asked for assistance in locating her missing fiancé, one George Shen."

VII

On Monday morning Edward Kennelly, Detective Captain, District police, and Robert Kirkwal, Agent, Secret Service, were sworn in as commanders, United States Navy Reserve, by Frank Knox, Secretary of the Navy. They barely had time to receive congratulations. They knew that the First Lady had something important for them at the White House.

"The President trusts us with this," she said, handing them a message from Chungking. "It was decoded and hand delivered to the President about an hour ago."

The message read—

PRESIDENT OF THE UNITED STATES
For His Eyes Only

This replies, Sir, to your message of inquiry relative to certain members of the staff traveling with Madame Chiang Kai-shek.

I am personally acquainted with T'sa Yuang-hung. He is a captain in the Kuomintang Intelligence Service. I have found him competent, intelligent, and of course utterly amoral and ruthless. His presence in the Chiang party can only signify that Madame Chiang has her own reasons to be accompanied by a tough bodyguard.

Liang P'ing is a professional criminal, a type that I must unhappily report seems to characterize a significant element of the inner circle around the Generalissimo. Liang has a long arrest record, dating back to 1932 when he was, reputedly, the keeper of a string of bordellos on the Shanghai waterfront. He has served time in prison for such crimes as extortion, armed robbery, and assault also bribery and corruption of public officials.

Weng Guo-fang is one of the last of the eunuchs who served at the old Imperial Court. You may regard him as a skilled professional survivor. He is in his seventies and has landed on his feet through all kinds of times and adventures. He is unequivocally Machiavellian. You must not, of course, trust him. I very much doubt even the Chiangs do. On the other hand, I am sure they rely on him for his shrewd insights into people and events.

I don't know who the maids might be—particularly since you didn't name them. I would be very much surprised, though, if one of them does not service Liang P'ing.

I regret, Mr. President, that you find these kinds of people your guests in the White House. I am sure both of us would like to avoid their ilk. Please advise me if I can be of any further service.

Stilwell, Lieutenant General

"Is it possible," Mrs. Roosevelt asked, "that Mr. T'sa Yuang-hung, a Chinese intelligence agent, recognized Mr. Shen as a spy and—"

"Is it possible," Kennelly interrupted, "that Shen somehow owed money to Liang P'ing and—"

"Neither thesis explains how Shen got into the White House, nor why he was here," said Kirkwal.

"What we do know is that the Chiang entourage is a nest of vipers," said Kennelly. "Diplomatic status or no, Madame Chiang's staff or no, I'll lay money that one of those two Chinks had something to do with the murder of Shen. There are too many coincidences here."

"Let me add one more," said Mrs. Roosevelt. "Miss Chin Yu-lin went to the San Francisco police yesterday and reported Mr. Shen was missing. She asked their assistance in finding him."

"I'd like to interview *her,*" said Kennelly.

"You will," said the First Lady. "The President has arranged for her to fly to Washington on a military flight. She will be here this evening."

At noon Mrs. Roosevelt and Harry Hopkins were the guests of a delegation of union leaders who had come to Washington to coordinate their efforts to convince the administration that wage increases should be allowed, to overcome the effects of inflation. Present at the luncheon were Philip Murray, president of the C.I.O.; William Green, president of the A.F. of L.; Walter Reuther, president of the United Auto Workers; and Sidney Hillman, president of the Amalgamated Clothing Workers. Also present was A. Philip Randolph, president of the Brotherhood of Sleeping Car Porters, whose agenda included much more than just inflation and wages. John L. Lewis was in the hotel, but he was presiding over a separate luncheon of officers of the United Mine Workers and some dissident officers of the Brotherhood of Railroad Trainmen.

For a long time Mrs. Roosevelt had enjoyed a more cordial relationship with the leaders of organized labor than did the President himself. President Roosevelt was a pragmatic man. He had his ideals, but he knew he could do very little to bring them to reality if he did not win elections. His reaction to A. Philip Randolph had been consistent: He would do what he could for the Negro people, but if he did all they asked of him he would lose the electoral votes of the South and would no longer be President—and did they think Alfred Landon or Wendell Willkie would have done even as much as he had done to secure their rights? The same with labor. He was the friend of labor. They couldn't deny it. But if he indulged their wage demands in the middle of war and inflation, what he allowed them would be taken away by Congress—taken away in fact by the outrage of the American people, who would see striking union men as wartime traitors and would demand drastic action against them.

Mrs. Roosevelt, over the years, had become more committed to the interests of labor, as a philosophical matter. Women like Rose Schneiderman, head of the Women's Trade Union League, had taught Eleanor Roosevelt to think of unions as instruments for social justice, not just as organizations that might deliver votes.

Labor leaders understood this. So did Republicans of the Right, who sincerely regarded the wife of the President as a dangerous ideologue. The fact that she attended this luncheon was ideologically significant, and she knew that some of tomorrow's newspapers would editorially note her presence at this meeting.

Actually, the luncheon with the labor leaders was uneventful. They stated their positions, knowing she would carry their word back to the President. They had a good point, she told them. But she added that she hoped they would not sacrifice the long-term respect of the American people for short-term advantages.

"Millions of American families have sons and brothers, fathers, uncles, cousins, serving in the armed forces and facing imminent danger of life," she said. "If they were to gain the impression that you would impede the industrial production that provides those men and boys the weapons they need to survive, for a few cents an hour in wages, *you* will be the ultimate losers—and your loss will be major and tragic."

In the hotel lobby as she walked toward the exit and her waiting car, she encountered John L. Lewis. He asked her if she could spare him a few minutes. She said yes. She did not see how she could deny him.

He took her—and Harry Hopkins—to the best suite in the hotel, where he offered them whiskey from silver decanters. Hopkins accepted. Mrs. Roosevelt did not.

John Llewellyn Lewis was, depending

on your point of view, one of the greatest Americans of the century, a brave, fierce, and determined fighter for one of America's most brutally exploited underclasses, the coal miners—or a coarse, narrow-minded fanatic who cared little about what happened to his country so long as the miners he represented got what they wanted and continued to afford him money and power.

A burly, scowling man with a theatrical shock of thick brown hair, now turning gray, shaggy, dramatically mobile eyebrows, an elephantine lower lip, and a rumbling voice that could and did propel echoing thunders of scorn on any who dared oppose him, John L. Lewis was a menacing figure. Indeed, he had once terminated a scathing personal attack on his integrity by stepping up to the podium and felling the speaker with a destructive blow to the jaw. The President himself had not been spared the lash of the Lewis tongue.

"The *operators* . . ." he said, when they were seated in his suite. (Operators was the term for coal-mine owners, and he could hardly speak the word without a sneer.) "The operators carry off obscene profits while the miners, who work in ever-present imminent danger of injury or death, continue to live in squalor. You have visited some of their humble homes, Eleanor—and so have you, Harry—and you would be appalled, I swear, to see that they still live as they did, while production and profits have soared through the ceiling and the roof and ascend toward the clouds."

"Surely, Mr. Lewis," she said. "Surely you cannot be contemplating a strike. How can you think of disrupting industrial production in that major way when so many of our men are— "

"*My* men struggle every day, all their lives, in trenches no less dangerous, on the average day, than the trenches wherein soldiers await attack or prepare for the charge. Most soldiers will survive. Most miners will not."

"Really— " said Hopkins.

Lewis grabbed away Hopkins's glass and poured more whiskey over his ice. "Statistics, Harry," he said. "The life expectancy of a combat infantryman in time of war is greater than that of a coal miner in time of peace."

"A miner is paid many times the pay of a combat infantryman," said Hopkins.

"Aha! If you were twenty-five years younger, Harry, which would you rather be—a combat infantryman in the muddy trenches before Belleau Wood, with a chance you might die in the next twenty-four hours, or a coal miner condemned to labor in dark and damp and dust—and constant fear—in the midst of poison gasses, in a cramped underground tunnel that might collapse at any moment, and face years and years of that labor, in the certainty, not the possibility but the *certainty,* you will die young from what that kind of labor does to a man's lungs and heart."

"You make a dramatic case," said Hopkins.

"I make a truthful case," rumbled Lewis.

"We were speaking of a strike," said Mrs. Roosevelt. "Surely, in time of war—"

"American soldiers," said Lewis, "went to war only from December 1941. The miners have lived with wartime conditions all their lives."

"The President really can't permit a strike," she said.

"Oh, yes. He's going to bring in the army, to make us dig coal. Can bayonets at their backs make my men dig coal, Eleanor?"

"I hope we shall not have to find out, Mr. Lewis," she said. "I very much hope we shall not have to find out."

Shortly before noon, T'sa Yuang-hung left the White House. He was a compact, muscular man whom Mrs. Roosevelt had judged to be in his late thirties. Leaving by the north gate, he walked across Pennsylvania Avenue and into Lafayette Park. There he found a park bench and sat down. Bundled in a black wool overcoat against the chill of February, he sat and watched the bustle and traffic of downtown Washington.

Since his arrival in the United States, he had spent what time he could this way, alone, observing, gaining what impressions he could of the strange, powerful nation America was. He had sat in Central Park in New York and stared at Americans. He had walked the streets of that city. He had come to Washington from New York by train, staring from the train windows at the vast industrial complexes of New Jersey that you could see from the railroad. Now he was in Washington. The city was like New York: lively, buoyant, filled with optimism.

The war had hardly touched America. These energetic cities had not been bombed, had never been threatened by invasion or occupation, had not known fear or hunger—and, what was more, they didn't expect to. Madame Chiang had said it was so. He had not believed her.

It was obvious that the key to the war lay here. No matter what anyone did in Asia, the key lay here. If a man was to make a contribution to victory, he had to make it here. The Chiangs knew it. That was why the Madame was here.

That was why *he* was here.

An elderly gentleman—white-haired, wearing spectacles, wearing also a black overcoat and gray hat—sat down on the other end of the bench. He glanced at T'sa Yuang-hung and smiled vaguely. Then he opened a white paper bag and began to toss crumbs and nuts to the birds.

After a while the gentleman smiled

again and said, "They expect me. I suspect it spoils their day when I don't come."

"That bag of crumbs and nuts would feed a Chinese child for the day," said T'sa Yuang-hung.

"Chinese? Yes. It *would* feed a Chinese child. Or a Russian one. The problem is, we need to feed ten million Chinese children. Ten million. Ten million Russian children. And how would we manage to ship tens of millions of bags of crumbs and nuts to China or Russia?" The old man shook his head. "In the meantime, I shall feed a bit to the birds and squirrels."

"You are not inhumane," said T'sa Yuang-hung.

"Oh, God, I should hope not. You are Chinese. Not just Chinese-American, but—"

"A member of the personal staff accompanying Madame Chiang Kai-shek."

The old man nodded. In fact, T'sa Yuang-hung took his solemn nod for a faint bow.

"Give Madame Chiang my regards," he said. "My name is Bernard Baruch. I think she will know the name."

" 'Bernard Baruch,' " T'sa Yuang-hung repeated. "I will tell her."

A few minutes later, the Chinese intelligence officer left the bench. He bowed to Baruch and walked east, out of the park and onto the streets of downtown Washington.

He had carefully committed to memory a map of the streets in the immediate vicinity of the White House. He knew that if he walked northeast on New York Avenue, he would come to H Street. (The Americans, astonishingly, called the streets in their nation's capitol city by such names as First, Second, Third, A, B, C, and so on. Had the nation no heroes?) East on H Street he would enter a neighborhood where the Chinese citizens of the city congregated in a small area. That was his target.

Though it was called a Chinatown, the neighborhood was tiny, nothing like the Chinatowns in San Francisco and New York. The streets were typical though: lined with small restaurants, laundries, and little stores selling Chinese food specialties, tea, spices, incense, and kaleidoscopic bric-a-brac. Almost every storefront bore a sign declaring in large letters that this place was CHINESE—meaning it was not Japanese.

He found the store he was looking for. SHANGHAI IMPORT COMPANY, the sign said, in gold letters on the window. He opened the door. Hanging bells clanged.

The air of the store was heavy with mixed fragrances: those of tea, spices, and Chinese medicinal roots and herbs. Paper lanterns hung from the ceiling. Teakwood boxes inlaid with mother-of-pearl sat on teakwood tables. Small figures carved from jade grimaced from inside locked glass cabinets. In another glass cabinet sat an ivory boat. Prints hung from the walls.

Shanghai Import Company was, in short, just what an American wanted to see when he came into a Chinese store. It was the opposite of a tourist trap. The store was the tourist, and it trapped the locals, instead of the locals trapping the tourists.

A man came out from the rear and stood behind a glass showcase where objects liked carved big-bellied gods, brass incense burners, and little brass bells were on display.

T'sa Yuang-hung spoke to him, in Chinese. "Greetings to you. I am T'sa Yuang-hung."

"Greetings. I am called Henry K'ang. I have been expecting you."

Henry K'ang was a smaller man than T'sa Yuang-hung, yet probably weighed more. His flat face was broad, his mouth wide and thin-lipped. His hair was turning gray. He wore thick rimless eyeglasses.

"Can we talk?"

The man shrugged. "Why not?"

T'sa Yuang-hung glanced around the store, as if dissatisfied with the man's assurance and unsure if they could be overheard.

"Relax, my friend," said Henry K'ang. "If I could not be confident of the security of this place, I would not be here."

"Then I can report that all is in perfect order."

"*Perfect order* is a pregnant phrase. *Perfect* is a very big word."

"We have but one problem," said T'sa Yuang-hung.

"Liang P'ing."

"Yes."

"Yes. When one deals with a pimp—"

"Worse than a pimp," said T'sa Yuang-hung. "More than a pimp."

"You need not tell me the nature of the problem. I am not surprised. When the Generalissimo and Madame Chiang allow such people to attend on them, they must expect troubles."

"We have had his cooperation until now."

"Until he saw his opportunity."

"I suppose so."

"His kind never cease to look for opportunity," said Henry K'ang scornfully.

"He was not born at a respectable social level," said T'sa Yuan-hung.

"Let him come to see me," said Henry K'ang. "After all, he *must* see me if he wants to do what I imagine he wants to do."

"It may not be easy to persuade him to leave the White House."

"I am certain you will persuade him."

Chin Yu-lin knew her fiancé was dead. She had been told so in San Francisco very early this morning, before she was told she was to fly to Washington and visit the White House. She'd had time to compose herself. Entering the White House, led through the North Portico, she was distracted from her grief, by the magnificence of the Cross Hall. Then, to her amazement, she was led between two flags and into a beautiful oval-shaped room. It was the Blue Room, and the wife of the President of the United States waited for her there.

She had been met at the airport by a handsome Secret Service agent named Kirkwal, and he had carried her bags to his car and into the White House. She had been told she would be given a room in the White House during her stay.

Chin Yu-lin was mystified.

Mrs. Roosevelt had intended she should be. It would be advantageous, she had decided, to make the small Chinese girl feel important. It was important to encourage her to speak frankly and tell the truth.

The First Lady came toward her, arms outstretched, a welcoming smile on her face. "Oh, my dear," she said. "I am so sorry about the bad news you've had."

Chin Yu-lin had not imagined Mrs. Roosevelt could be so tall. She herself was only five-feet-two, and the First Lady towered over her: a big, kindly-looking woman, also more attractive than Chin Yu-lin had supposed, certainly not deserving of the cruel jokes that were made about her appearance.

The Chinese girl was just nineteen years old. She was modestly dressed in a black jacket, white blouse, black skirt. Her skirt was the "patriotic" length—short. Her legs were bare—as were the legs of most young women and girls in the winter of 1942–43, when nylon stockings had all but disappeared from the stores. She wore short white socks that just covered her ankles. Petite though she was, she had a full figure: heavy bust, broad hips, and short sturdy legs. Her face looked squashed, as many Chinese faces did to Western eyes. It was short and wide, and looked even more so since she wore her black hair in bangs almost to her eyebrows. To Mrs. Roosevelt it seemed a face that must usually have been broadened even more, with a happy smile—though she wore no smile tonight. She chewed gum, and her slowly moving jaw somehow lent an added measure of solemnity to her face.

Kirkwal could not help compare what he had seen of Chin Yu-lin since he met her coming off the airplane to what he had seen in her nude photo that had been among the possessions of the late George Shen.

"Miss Chin, have you had dinner?"

"No, Ma'am."

"Then let's go somewhere comfortable and order some. Mr. Kirkwal, you've not had yours either, I imagine."

From the private dining room, Mrs. Roosevelt called down an order for two dinners, also coffee. She asked Kirkwal if he would like to have a drink of whiskey, and he said he would.

"Well, Miss Chin, that won't take long. Dinner will be up in a few minutes. I should imagine you are tired. We do have some questions to ask you about Mr. Shen, but really they can wait until morning."

"I can talk now," said Chin Yu-lin.

"You've been told that Mr. Shen was murdered," the First Lady began gently.

Chin Yu-lin nodded.

Mrs. Roosevelt hesitated for a moment, then said, "I'm sorry to have to tell you this, but there is good reason to think he was a Japanese spy."

The girl shifted her chewing gum. "I figured somethin' like that, when they told me I had to come to Washington. But I don't know nothin' about it. If he was a spy, it's news to me."

"We accept that. But did you have any reason to suspect him? What sort of man was he, dear? What can you tell us about him?"

"My family didn't want me to marry him. They figured he was too old for me."

"He was forty-one," said Kirkwal.

Chin Yu-lin shook her head. "Thirty-four."

"His driver's license says he was forty-one. His draft registration says he was forty-one."

"Maybe the son of a bitch lied to me."

"How long had you known him?" asked Mrs. Roosevelt.

The girl chewed her gum more vigorously. It snapped. " 'Bout a year."

"What did he do for a living?"

"Sold shoes."

"For whom? For what company?"

Chin Yu-lin shrugged. Then she raised a finger and said, "Okay, he sold the kind I've got on. He brought them to me. Samples, he said." She reached down and took off a low-heeled black shoe. "Enna-Jetticks," she said, reading from the label.

Kirkwal nodded. He would check with the company.

"He'd been a Japanese interpreter before," said Mrs. Roosevelt.

"And had made a lot more money."

"Did he ever visit Japan?"

The girl shrugged. "Not that I know of."

Chin Yu-lin opened her little purse, took out a pack of cigarettes, and used a Zippo to light a Camel.

"But he spoke fluent Japanese?"

"S'pose so, if he worked as an interpreter."

"But you don't know where he learned it? Or how?"

"What about Chinese?" Kirkwal asked. "Did he speak good Chinese?"

"Don't ask me," said Chin Yu-lin. "I don't know more'n twenty words. He talked Chinese to my father." She snickered. "He talks a big case, but he can't speak it, either. My grandfather . . . Well, he said George talked Chinese with a horrible accent. But my grandfather's from Canton. Far as he's concerned, anybody that don't talk Cantonese don't talk Chinese."

"In your letter to Shen . . ." Kirkwal began. "Well, I'm sorry, Miss Chin, but he was carrying a letter from you when he died. You—"

The girl choked back a sob and wiped her eyes that filled with tears. She took a deep drag on her cigarette and looked around for an ashtray. Mrs. Roosevelt passed her a small plate.

"In your letter you express some contempt for Madame Chiang Kai-shek. Do you—"

"Madam Peanut," said Chin Yu-lin with bitter scorn. "General Peanut. They press Chinese families in this country to give them money. Hey . . . My family could care less if the Japs caught Peanut and hung him. Her, too. And took over the whole country. The Chinese in the part occupied by Japan are just as well off as the people in the part controlled by Chiang. You know what a tong is? It's a Chinese gang. Chinese gangsters. That's all the Peanut is: just another tong chief."

"Did Mr. Shen feel this way?" asked Mrs. Roosevelt.

An usher came in with a bottle of bourbon on a tray—with ice, soda, and glasses. Kirkwal poured himself a bourbon and soda. Chin Yu-lin pointed at the bottle, and he poured her a drink, too.

"George . . . George hardly talked about politics. Hey! George had a zoot suit! Never wore it much, but he had it. George was a hip guy. Hip to the jive, you know? Forty-one years old, you say? Jesus!"

"Maybe you didn't know much about him, really," Kirkwal suggested.

"Maybe I didn't. Maybe I just didn't."

"Will you stay with us a few days, dear?" asked Mrs. Roosevelt. "As my guest, here in the White House?"

"I got any choice?"

"Certainly. You're not being detained. Not by any means. If you want, we'll put you on a plane back to San Francisco in the morning."

Chin Yu-lin lifted her glass and took a drink of whiskey and soda. "Guest in the White House . . ." she mused. *"Me?* Jeez! Lady, I'll live here the rest of the war, if that's what you want. Wait'll my mama hears about this!"

VIII

Madame Chiang joined Mrs. Roosevelt for breakfast in the private dining room on Tuesday morning. For the first time since her arrival at the White House she was not dressed in black but was wearing jade green: the usual form-fitting silk dress with high collar and slit skirt. On the way down to the dining room, she said she felt better, more energetic, that she seemed to be recovering nicely from the surgery that had been done in New York.

The First Lady had invited three distinguished guests for breakfast: Senator Harry Truman, because she felt Madame Chiang had not appreciated at the formal dinner on Thursday evening that Truman might have a good deal to say in Congress about how much more aid would be appropriated; Bernard Baruch, because she wanted his appraisal of Madame Chiang; and Speaker of the House Sam Rayburn, who had been invited for Thursday night but had pleaded a prior commitment.

Baruch had a small office in the East Wing and was an official adviser to the President—without compensation—but he rarely visited the office and was more often to be found sitting on his park bench across the street. He had been a college boxer, and though he was now seventy-three years old, Baruch was still an erect and sturdy man. His hair was thick and white. A pince-nez sat astride his nose. His square face was a little flushed.

Senator Truman was a bouncy, peppery man, quick to smile, quick to scowl. As chairman of a Senate committee that had come to be known as the Truman Committee, he was in charge of investigating cost overruns and possible fraud in defense contracts. His work had given him a nationwide reputation. He had in fact risen above his origins in the Missouri political machine of boss Tom Pendergast and had far exceeded the President's expectations of him.

Sam Rayburn was of course the squat, bullet-headed Texan he had always been. Since he succeeded Speaker Bankhead three years ago, he had proved to be a tough and effective leader of the Democrats in Congress.

"I'm sorry the President can't join us," said Senator Truman.

"Harry," said Mrs. Roosevelt. "He is still in bed. But let us not suppose he is sleeping. This is the time when he eats his breakfast, reviews the newspapers, and receives members of his personal staff with urgent demands for presidential decisions. Mr. Churchill makes important decisions at two or three in the morning—then sleeps until long after the President is awake and active. A matter of personal style."

"I can remember many and many a morning," said Senator Truman, "when I saw the ol' sun come up over the tail ends of a pair of mules. A man can do some awful good work about the time the sun rises."

Mrs. Roosevelt saw Madame Chiang frown for an instant and lift her chin, at these words. A daughter of the Soong dynasty knew nothing about working in the fields—at any hour.

"A man that can watch the sun come up over a pair of mules that are pullin' his plow is a lucky man," said Sam Rayburn. "I've known farmers that'd give anything for the privilege. I wonder, Madame Chiang, what plans your husband has to redistribute the land in China after the war—so every farmer can have his mite."

For the first time since she'd met the First Lady of China, the First Lady of the United States saw Madame Chiang flustered. She saw also that the First Lady of China did not like being confronted with a question for which she did not have a graceful answer.

"You must understand," said Madame Chiang, "that China has many centuries-old problems that do not readily lend themselves to the kinds of solutions that are applicable in America."

"It'd help," said Senator Truman, "if not so many people stole so damned much."

Madame Chiang hardened. "Who steals, Senator?" she asked. "Who, specifically?"

He shrugged. "From what I hear, everybody who can. From what I hear, ten percent—no, twenty or twenty-five percent—of our aid winds up in somebody's pockets. Not embezzlement. Not graft. Downright theft."

Madame Chiang smiled at him. "You have my personal invitation, Senator, to come to China—and I hope you will come as soon as possible—to look into this question on your own. It distresses me to think that a prominent United States Senator holds us in so low regard."

"It's not personal, Madame," said Senator Truman, "and I don't have to come look to know. I just want to see our aid dollars do as much good for your country as possible."

"As do we, Senator. As do we."

"A statement of democratic principles might go a long way to persuade members of Congress," said Senator Truman.

"I am reminded," said Madame Chiang, "of an old story told about a Buddhist monk and a Christian missionary. It happened in Tibet. The missionary, aboard an ass, came upon the monk sitting in the dust by the side of the road. And the monk was chanting—'Om mani padme hum. Om mani padme hum.' This translates—'The Jewel in the Lotus, Amen. The Jewel in the Lotus, Amen.' As the missionary approached, the monk kept up his chant—'*Om mani padme hum. Om mani padme hum.*' The missionary stopped. 'My brother,' he said, 'What are these words?' The monk replied, 'These words are a prayer, a mantra as the Hindus would say. *Om mani padme hum. Om mani padme hum.* Reciting these words endlessly, throughout life, is the supreme act of grace. *Om mani padme hum. Om mani padme hum.*' And the missionary said, 'Oh, my brother, sitting and chanting is not truly an act of grace. You do not achieve grace by repeating your prayer but by acting on it. God notes, not how just many times you say your prayer, but how you live your life.' So, you see, Senator, I would rather be judged, not by the ideals we proclaim, but by the ideals we *live.*"

"Somethin' screwball," said Ed Kennelly.

"No surprise, I'd think," said Kirkwal.

"Let's ask the Chink girl what *she* thinks," said Kennelly.

Chin Yu-lin appeared a few minutes later in the Secret Service office on the ground floor of the White House. She wore a flowered dress and was smoking a cigarette.

"Shoes . . ." said Kirkwal. "Enna-Jetticks never heard of a George Shen. Neither have the companies that wholesale Enna-Jetticks shoes on the West Coast."

"What does that make me?" asked Chin Yu-lin.

"A charming young girl that was lied to," said Kennelly. "Mrs. Roosevelt's not here, so let's get some things straight. You were puttin' out to this guy, right?"

She shrugged. "So? You goin' to send me to a federal pokey for that? You better have some damned big pokeys all set up, 'cause there's millions of us."

"Was he really going to marry you?" asked Kennelly.

"Of course he—" She stopped. For a brief moment she confronted the big Irish detective, her face dark with anger. Then she took a drag from her cigarette and shrugged. "Who knows?" she asked glumly.

"He worked for Occident and Orient Steamship Lines until the war came," said Kirkwal. "O and O confirms that. They let him go because they had no more need for a Japanese interpreter. He was unemployed from January of 1942 until he died here last week. What was he living on, Yu-lin? *How* did he live? Was he rich, or poor, or what?"

"Lived like an ordinary sort of guy. Hey. He lived like a guy that sold shoes for a living. Okay?"

"I'm gonna ask you something, Yu-lin," said Kennelly. "I get the idea that you're a pretty smart girl. You know the score. What about George? Was he smart? Smart as you?"

Her chin rose, and she tipped her head to one side. "What you drivin' at, Kennelly?"

"Never mind what I'm driving at. I get an impression. I get an impression of a sharp young girl—pretty, sexy, knows the score—getting ready to marry a guy that wasn't in her class. What's the deal?"

Chin Yu-lin ground out her cigarette in an ashtray on the desk. "What'd you grow up in, Kennelly? Irish family? Try an Italian family. And if an Irish or Italian family doesn't smother you, try a Chinese family. He was going to set up a home for us, some way, somehow; and we were going to live like grownups; and I was going to tell my Chinese ancestors to go to hell. Okay?"

"You knew damn well he didn't sell shoes for a living," said Kennelly.

"Well, I didn't think he was any spy."

"What'd you think he was?"

"Lots of guys makes a living just being smart."

"George?"

"Well . . ."

"He wasn't smart enough to make a living just being smart," said Kennelly. "You had to know he was working for somebody. Doing something. Doing what, dammit?"

"Little red pills, I figured," said Chin Yu-lin.

Kennelly glanced at Kirkwal, who raised his eyebrows as he returned his glance.

"Explain that one, kid," said Kennelly.

"C'mon," she sneered. "The whole world's full of them."

Kennelly shook his head. "Keep talkin'. And let's get something straight, Yu-lin. Mrs. R may be a kind and gentle lady, but Bobby and I got authority to rack your little ass into a cold steel cell in D.C. police headquarters. We're investigating a murder, and if we get any idea you're giving us anything but full cooperation, you won't sleep another night in the White House; you'll start sleeping nights behind bars."

"It's a *guess!*" she protested. "He never mentioned any little red pills."

"Tell us about little red pills," said Kirkwal.

Her hands trembled as she shook a Camel from her pack and lit it with her Zippo. "Jeez Christ, fellas. You wanta tell me you don't know? Look— When the goddamn Japs took over most of China, they also took over most of the opium fields. Five years ago, like. They got factories. They turn the opium into— You know."

"Heroin," said Kennelly.

"And like," she said. "I don't know what's in the little red pills, exactly. Heroin or morphine. Something like. They make millions of little red pills, every year. They pour 'em into China and places, free. The soldiers take the pills and don't feel like fighting. Other places, they sell 'em, which makes money they can use for all kinds of things."

"How come you know about what we don't know about?" Kennelly asked.

"Can I help it if *you're* stupid? You ask the 'Frisco cops. They know all about it. Ask army intelligence. They know about it."

"Are you saying these pills are coming into the United States," Kirkwal asked.

"Ask the 'Frisco police. Ask the FBI."

"And you figure George Shen was selling these little red pills?"

She shook her head. "I figure, more likely, he got in the way of somebody who was. That's why I went to the cops."

"And because you figure, if somebody triggered him, they might come for you next," said Kennelly.

"Hey . . . If somebody had it all that screwed up—"

Kennelly stood up and towered over her. "Straight talk, little girl. You're in one kind of deep shit. Better not get in another."

She looked up at him. She drew a deep breath. "When George didn't come back, I went to his room. I had a key. I searched. I mean, I was lookin' for little red pills."

"You find any?"

She nodded. "Seventeen of 'em. Exactly seventeen. I poured 'em out and counted them." She shook her head. "He wasn't selling them. He was *taking* them."

"What did you do with them?"

"I flushed 'em down the john. That was my first idea, to get rid of the damned things. Whether he came back or not."

"Then—"

"Well, that told me he was mixed up with some rough guys. And that's why I went to the cops."

"Do you believe her?" asked Mrs. Roosevelt.

"About as far as I could throw her," said Kennelly.

"The pills taken from his room were just aspirin," said Kirkwal. "White pills."

"This complication offers nothing by way of explanation of Mr. Shen's presence in the White House," said Mrs. Roosevelt. "Nothing to explain his death."

"It's possible that Chin Yu-lin has some motive for trying to muddy the waters," said Kirkwal. "She's not a very nice young woman, Ma'am."

Mrs. Roosevelt smiled. " 'Not *our* sort of young woman,' " the President's mother would have said.

"I'd count the spoons with a guest like that in the White House," said Kennelly.

The First Lady smiled. "Mrs. Nesbitt is counting the ones used to serve Madame Chiang and her people. I'm afraid half the kitchen staff are engaged in counting spoons."

Kirkwal grinned. "Ah," he said—

> " 'Which I wish to remark,—
> And my language is plain,—
> That for ways that are dark,
> And for tricks that are vain,
> The heathen Chinee is peculiar,—
> Which the same I would rise to
> explain.' "

Mrs. Roosevelt laughed. "Oh, Mr. Kirkwal, I had hoped to get through this visit from the Madame without hearing that verse."

"I am sorry."

"Not at all. It has been running through my head from the day she arrived."

Kennelly smiled and frowned at the same time. He was amused by the verse but had never heard it before.

"I've another problem," said Mrs. Roosevelt, her mien shifting to sober. "Madame Chiang told me after breakfast this morning that her man Liang P'ing left the White House last evening some time and has not as yet returned. That is, he had not yet returned when she asked for him this morning."

"The Shanghai pimp," said Kennelly. "She might think of herself as well shed of him."

"We can't look at it that way," said the First Lady.

"No, of course not."

"He had to go out through a gate," said Kirkwal. "And a note would have been made in the gate log. I'll check with Major Bentz."

Major Bentz had the record. Liang P'ing had left the White House at 8:58 P.M.

on Monday. There was no record to indicate he had returned.

"Do Madame's staff go in and out much?" Kirkwal asked.

"The old man, Weng Guo-fang, goes in and out. T'sa Yuang-hung, the male secretary, has been out only once. That was yesterday morning. He was gone about two hours. Liang P'ing went out just one time before he left last night. That was last Wednesday afternoon. He was with the old man. The others have never left the White House since they arrived last Wednesday."

On their way back through the White House, Kirkwal and Kennelly stopped in the kitchen for a cup of coffee. An usher named George was in attendance there, ready to carry upstairs any orders for coffee or food that might come down. The Chinese guests, he said, ordered hot water and tea leaves. They insisted on brewing their own tea, in their rooms.

Kirkwal and Kennelly sat at the big kitchen table, where lunch preparations were about to begin, and sipped mugs of black coffee.

"Pills . . ." said Kennelly. "If she's telling the truth and he only had seventeen on hand, she's probably right that he was taking them, not selling them."

"But," said Kirkwal, "if they're what she says they are—that is, alkaloids of opium—they're addictive. If he was taking them, he'd want some every day. So why didn't we find any on him or in his room?"

"Maybe we oughta go back out to Mrs. Forsythe's boardinghouse and take a closer look at that room," said Kennelly.

Mrs. Forsythe had already rented Shen's room to another man. His personal possessions were stored in a big closet in the cellar of the house. His clothes and toiletries were all neatly packed in his two suitcases.

She offered the two men the use of her laundry room, where they could open Shen's bags on her laundry table and search them more thoroughly. She did not want to watch them, she said, and left them to their labors.

They now began the process of examining the pockets and linings of every item of Shen's clothing. It would have been easy for him to pour a substantial supply of little red pills into the lining of a jacket, or to push them into the lining of the waistband of a pair of trousers; and the only way to find them was to finger every square inch of the three jackets in his bags, plus the waistbands of five pairs of pants.

"I'm going to want to wash my hands when I finish this," said Kirkwal.

"Police work," said Kennelly. "Dirtier than Secret Service work."

"Coolidge used to like to go out and grub around in the fields, pretend he was a farmer," said Kirkwal. "We'd get all muddy following him. One time he took a pitchfork and began to toss hay into a wagon. He wanted me to do the same. You get damned sweaty, doing that in a three-piece suit."

"Why'd he want to do that?"

"For the cameras, of course. Why'd you suppose?"

They worked on, until Kennelly said, "Wild-goose chase. I don't feel any pills."

"Me neither. But there's something in this pair of pants. And look here. This lining's been slit. See, there's a hole in it."

"What are you feeling?"

"Not pills," said Kirkwal, ". . . paper."

Kennelly pulled a small, horn-handled folding knife from his pocket. He pulled up a blade that had a pointed tip and shoved that blade into the slit in the lining. With a wrenching move, he cut stitches then ripped the fabric away.

"Money!"

New bills. Fifties. Cutting and ripping, they tore away the lining and pulled the money out on Mrs. Forsythe's laundry table. Sixteen fifty-dollar bills.

But no matter how much they searched, they found no little red pills.

"It makes no sense. No sense at all," Kirkwal said to Mrs. Roosevelt an hour later. "If he took the pills himself, he was an addict, and we should have found his supply. If he sold them, he would have had more than seventeen in San Francisco and more cash on him here in Washington. I mean, if he came here to sell pills, surely he would have made more than eight hundred dollars."

"Some of your reasoning depends on

our accepting the word of Miss Chin," said the First Lady.

"Yes, and I—"

"We do have confirmation of her judgment that he was taking the pills himself. Remember the autopsy report. It said he had ingested codeine or morphine in the seventy-two hours before his death."

"True."

"I believe, Mr. Kirkwal, we should concentrate our attention on the problem of how Mr. Shen invaded the White House and reached the second floor, then the problem of who murdered him in the Map Room and why."

"I wholly agree. The business of the pills is a side issue."

Mrs. Roosevelt shrugged and smiled. "A side issue that may, of course, hold the key to the whole mystery."

Madame Chiang spent hours every day soaking in the hot water of the oversized bathtub in her suite. Among the items of her luggage was an ornate board—teakwood with an inlaid pattern of leaves and flowers—that lay across the rims of the tub and held the newspapers, magazines, and books she read, plus her cigarettes and holder and lighter, some jars of cream, and a big snifter well filled with Napoleon brandy.

Both her maids and Miss Kung attended her—all three of them naked in obedience to her rule that no one came into her presence when she was naked who was not naked also.

"Aha! Aha!" she said to Miss Kung. "So General Wingate has driven into Burma at the head of a force he calls 'Chindits.' So there! Indian troops. So at last the cowardly Indians will contribute something."

Miss Kung knew her only function was to nod agreement with whatever Madame Chiang chose to say. She sat as far from the tub as she could and still be in the bathroom, on a small upholstered chair dragged in for her. These hours without clothes were always an ordeal for her. She was a modest young woman, and to be compelled to display her petite, boyish body naked, even if only in the presence of Madame and her maids, was torment for her. Madame seemed proud of her naked self, and maybe she had a right to be; but for Miss Kung nakedness was misery.

"Right? Right?"

They spoke Chinese, of course. Miss Kung nodded and agreed, "Yes, right."

"Is Little Father waiting?"

"Yes, Madame."

"Call him in."

Miss Kung stepped to the door and spoke to Weng Guo-fang, who was sitting in the room outside, smoking, reading, and waiting. He rose and came into the bathroom.

Madame Chiang knew what Miss Kung did not and was comfortable about his coming into her bathroom. He immeasurably increased the anguish of the humiliated Miss Kung, who never ceased to blush when he came in, no matter how many times it had happened.

"Is there any word about Liang P'ing?" asked Madame Chiang.

"No, Madame. He still has not returned."

"I mentioned him to Mrs. Roosevelt this morning. I am afraid we are going to have to go so far as to report him missing."

"The American authorities—?"

"—will help us find him. I dislike having to ask their help, as you do; but we cannot allow him to abandon his duties this way."

"I never trusted him, Madame."

"I suppose you never did. Nor did I. Nor did the Generalissimo. But he has been useful."

"Where could he be? What could he be doing?"

"Seeking profit," she said. "His kind always find ways to look for profit."

"When we recover him—"

"I am quite sure, learned Little Father, you have not forgotten how to slice the back of a bad servant with the lash."

"I have retained that skill, Madame."

"You will have my permission to use it, even here in the White House."

Weng Guo-fang had retained also a facility for hissing his words, and he demonstrated that facility a few minutes later when he faced T'sa Yuang-hung.

"It is not to be tolerated! He must be returned!"

T'sa Yuang-hung nodded respect-fully—so formal a nod it was almost an old-fashioned bow.

"Do you understand? He cannot be permitted to abandon his duty. *Cannot!*"

"I understand."

"Whatever has to be done."

"Whatever," T'sa Yuang-hung re-peated.

IX

Malvina "Tommy" Thompson was often referred to by the First Lady as "the person who makes life possible for me." On Wednesday morning, Madame Chiang asked Tommy to sit down with her for a few minutes to discuss travel arrangements. Madame Chiang was planning a long tour of the United States before she returned to China, and she wanted some information about how the wife of the President of the United States traveled.

They met in Madame's suite, while Madame Chiang was eating her breakfast. She offered Tommy a cup of tea and plainly regarded that as a kind concession made to a servant. She did not suggest that the First Lady's secretary should partake of the ham and eggs, toast and marmalade, that were *her* breakfast.

Miss Kung, dressed as a man as

usual, sat a little apart, listening carefully to questions and answers.

"What staff accompanies Mrs. Roosevelt when she travels?"

Tommy Thompson had accompanied the First Lady on her visit to London and to the American bases in England and Scotland only a few months before, and they had traveled alone. Tommy was an experienced traveler as well as the close personal companion of the First Lady during her travels, and to some degree the question mystified her.

"Uh . . . Ordinarily, only I go with Mrs. Roosevelt when she travels—if in fact anyone at all goes with her. Lately, of course, a Secret Service agent, sometimes two, go along."

Madame Chiang Kai-shek smiled thinly. "I shall be carrying a staff of about forty persons during my tour of the United States," she said. "Am I really to believe that the wife of the President of the United States travels with fewer?"

Coiffed, manicured, perfumed, and wearing a flowered silk dress, Madame Chiang had drawn her tiny figure up into a posture of skepticism, even indignation.

Tommy didn't care what posture Madame assumed. She had made it plain to Mrs. Roosevelt that she despised the woman she regarded as arrogant, undemocratic, and a poseur.

"Miss Thompson, who packs the bags when Mrs. Roosevelt travels?"

"She packs her bags, and I pack mine."

Placid though her expression remained, it was plain on Madame Chiang's face that she didn't believe it. "Then who attends to such duties as pressing clothes?"

"Usually we stay in hotels. The hotel valet service takes care of things like that."

"Who answers the telephone?"

"Whoever is closer to it."

"Indeed . . ."

Tommy smiled. "Sometimes when Mrs. Roosevelt answers, she mimics my voice, until she finds out who is on the line. Then she says, 'I'm sorry but Mrs. Roosevelt is not available at the moment,' or she says, 'Yes, Mrs. Roosevelt is available,' holds the phone aside for a moment, and then answers in her own voice."

"Miss Thompson . . ."

"Mrs. Roosevelt is a very informal person."

"Very well," said Madame Chiang skeptically. "Very well. But you speak of two Secret Service agents. Who, really, is in charge of protecting Mrs. Roosevelt against would-be assassins?"

Tommy frowned. "Who would want to assassinate Mrs. Roosevelt?" she asked ingenuously. "The only problem we have is protecting her against too-enthusiastic people who want to rush up and embrace and kiss her."

"I see . . . Then, thank you Miss Thompson. I will not require any more of your time."

Captain Ed Kennelly telephoned Agent Bobby Kirkwal at 9:28 A.M.

"Got a new problem," he said. "You figure this business was as bad as it could get. Well, it just got worse."

In the few days they had worked together, Kirkwal had learned to read the nuances in Kennelly's voice. He had learned, besides, to respect the rough-hewn Washington cop as much as he had noticed the

First Lady did. He had heard exchanges between the two that told him they had worked together before, more than once. Right now he heard agitation and tension.

"What's the problem?"

"Some of the boys answered a call about two hours ago. A corpse floating in the Anacostia River, the caller said. And sure enough. They fished him out and made an identification. It's Madame Chiang's man Liang P'ing."

"Drowned?"

"Not unless he sank because water leaked in through the bullet holes."

"Uh-oh."

"Wanta have a look?"

"Do I have to?"

"Well, *I* have to. One good look before they cut him up for the autopsy."

"I'll notify Mrs. Roosevelt."

"I'll pick you up in twenty minutes."

The naked corpse of Liang P'ing lay on a stainless-steel table in the autopsy room at D.C. General Hospital. Having turned a sort of grayish blue, its skin color did not suggest that the small middle-aged man was Oriental.

"How long you figure he was in the water?" Kennelly asked the squat, late-middle-aged, chain-smoking doctor who had examined the body and was going to perform the autopsy.

"Twenty-four hours minimum," said Dr. Linus Englander. "Forty-eight max, but I don't think it was that long. I'd say he likely went in the water Monday night or early Tuesday morning. 'Course he didn't drown. He was dead when he went in."

The bullet holes were ghastly gray cavities. They had bled, and the river water had washed away every trace of blood. Liang P'ing had been shot in the chest, four times.

A uniformed officer came in. "You wanted to see me, Sir?" he said to Kennelly.

Kennelly nodded toward the corpse. "Anything special to tell us?"

"He was weighted down with a gunny sack full of rocks," said the policeman. "Tied to his ankle. 'Bout four feet of rope. But the current dragged him along, and when he went around that sharp curve in the river just inside the District line, the current moved him into shallow water, where that woman on the bank could see him."

"You figure he was put in the river out in Maryland?"

"Yes, sir. That'd be my guess."

"You have his clothes and personal stuff?"

"Yes, Sir. Got 'em spread out drying."

"Find anything unusual?"

"Chinese passport. A little over fifty dollars in money. No keys. No cigarettes. No lighter."

As this talk went on, the doctor had been manipulating the body with rubber-gloved hands, and now he said, "Be damned! Look at this, Kennelly. Whoever killed this bastard must have really wanted him dead. Besides being shot, he was conked on the head. Look at that!"

He pressed a finger into a shallow depression in the dead man's skull, at the top and rear.

"That's what you call skull fracture."

"You figure he was knocked unconscious and then shot?" Kennelly asked.

"Wouldn't be surprised. I want to get

them bullets out of him and get 'em to the ballistics boys. We won't be able to tell if he was shot first or conked first, but it wouldn't make much sense, would it, to shoot a man in the chest four times and *then* conk him on the head?"

"No," Kennelly agreed. "That wouldn't make much sense."

Dr. Englander ran a finger over the dead man's wrist. "Look at that, and look on his ankles."

The wrists and ankles were disfigured with shiny scars.

"You gotta figure," said the doctor, "that the fella was kept in chains for a long time. They do things like that in China, don't they?"

"He spent some time in a Chinese prison," said Kirkwal.

"Oh, so you know who he is?"

"Yes, we know who he is. And everything about him is a national-defense secret," said Kirkwal.

"Gotcha," said Dr. Englander. "Which means the autopsy report—"

"Just one copy," said Kennelly. "Which comes to me. And keep him here until we tell you what to do with him. He doesn't go to the morgue."

"Gotcha. Well . . . You wanta stick around and watch me cut him up?"

Kirkwal paled. Looking at the tools spread out on an adjacent table, he could guess without being told that the first thing the doctor was going to do was cut the chest and spread the two halves apart— very much like the way a diner cuts the body of a lobster on his plate. He didn't want to see that.

"I think Bobby'd rather not," said Kennelly with a grin. "And to be real honest with you, I guess I'd rather not myself."

"You don't know what you're missing," Dr. Englander chuckled.

"I deeply regret having to give you such news," said Mrs. Roosevelt.

She had sent word to Madame Chiang Kai-shek, asking her to come to the Green Room. It had seemed, somehow, that telling the woman that a member of her staff had been found dead, and not only dead but murdered, ought to be done in one of the formal rooms of the White House. Madame Chiang had come, bringing Weng Guo-fang with her.

"Shot . . ." murmured the grave old man.

Mrs. Roosevelt nodded. Kirkwal and Kennelly had not yet returned, and she knew only that Liang P'ing had been found in the Anacostia River, dead not of drowning but of gunshot wounds.

"Can the matter be kept quiet?" asked Madame Chiang.

"Yes," said the First Lady. "Entirely so."

"It is not a diplomatic incident," said Madame Chiang. "Liang P'ing left the White House, went somewhere, presumably to do something beyond the scope of his duties. He managed to get himself killed. I regret it, but I do not regard it as a matter of great concern. I hope you will not be troubled by it."

The autopsy report on Liang P'ing was delivered by messenger to Captain Kennelly at D.C. police headquarters. Shortly afterward, in mid-afternoon, he drove to the White House to deliver the document to Mrs. Roosevelt and Agent Kirkwal.

"I always dislike reading these things," said the First Lady. "Is there any reason why I must read it?"

"No, Ma'am. I can read you parts you might want to know about."

They sat in Mrs. Roosevelt's study on the second floor, where she had been dictating a newspaper column to Tommy Thompson until the big Irish detective arrived.

"Well . . ." said Kennelly as he flipped over the pages. "Here— 'The subject was killed by four shots from a firearm, presumably a pistol. (The sequence in which the bullets are below mentioned does not suggest the order in which they were fired.) One bullet shattered the ninth left rib, ruptured the spleen, passed through the colon, and exited through the rear of the thorax, causing a large exit wound. A second bullet was found wedged between the third and fourth dorsal vertebrae, whence it had come by penetration between two ribs and through the left lung, grazing and rupturing the pericardium. A third bullet was found in the left ventricle of the heart, together with a substantial quantity of bone splinters, which together had ruptured the ventricle. The fourth and last bullet was not found, but its path through the soft tissues of the thorax was clearly discernible. It had passed through the liver and left lung, causing major damage to both organs, and had exited through the muscle tissue and skin of the back, presumably continuing on through clothing. Any one of these bullets could have caused death, though clearly the second and third mentioned above would have caused death independently and rather quickly.' "

"I might as well be reading it," said Mrs. Roosevelt.

Kennelly continued—" 'In addition, the parietal bone of the skull is fractured, presumably by a violent blow from a blunt instrument, approximately one centimeter to the right of the sagittal suture. The fracture is approximately seven centimeters in length, approximately three in width, and the depth of the fracture at its deepest extremity is approximately two centimeters. The dura is ruptured, and a small quantity of bone debris has penetrated the parietal lobe of the brain. The blow that caused this injury would have rendered the subject unconscious, probably for an extended period of time.' "

"Does it appear that he was knocked unconscious and *then* shot?" asked Mrs. Roosevelt.

"Seems likely," said Kennelly. "Now . . ." He turned a page. "Going on. 'The subject had very likely engaged in sexual intercourse within the hour immediately preceding his death. Certainly he had experienced an ejaculation within that period. Entangled in the subject's pubic hair were six hairs not his own.' "

"A thorough autopsy," Mrs. Roosevelt remarked wryly.

"Not really," said Kennelly. "It's routine procedure to check for that."

"Is it?"

"Routine. Part of every autopsy I ever saw. Let me go on here— 'The subject had eaten heavily within the two hours preceding his death, a very substantial quantity of rice, fish, and chicken, with assorted vegetables. He had also ingested a substantial quantity of wine, also some gin. His blood-alcohol level was .13%"

"A vivid picture," said the First Lady. "Mr. Liang seems to have left the White House for the purpose of enjoying himself."

"He wasn't robbed," said Kennelly. "His property included $54.75 in cash. Also the stickpin in his necktie was a real diamond, a *big* real diamond."

"All this is consistent with what we know about him," said Mrs. Roosevelt. "He had been a criminal, what might be called a flashy character."

"With scars on his wrists and ankles from wearing chains in a Chinese prison," said Kirkwal.

"He was shot with a pistol we don't much see in this country," said Kennelly. "It's common enough in Europe. The Germans make it. It's called PPK, which stands for some German words; I don't know what. Anyway, it's what we'd call thirty-two caliber, and it's a pocket pistol. The marks on the bullets tell us they were fired from this Walther. They also tell us the pistol had never been used in a crime before—at least not in Washington and at least not where we recovered the slugs."

"So we know all about the murder of

Mr. Liang," said Mrs. Roosevelt. "We know everything except the small matter of who killed him and why."

Madame Chiang appointed T'sa Yuang-hung to receive all information about the death of Liang P'ing. Later in the afternoon he sat with Agent Kirkwal in the Secret Service office and heard all that Kennelly had reported to Mrs. Roosevelt.

"He was an evil man," said T'sa Yuang-hung. "Nothing but a criminal."

"If you don't mind my asking, why was a man like that on the personal staff of Madame Chiang Kai-shek?"

"The Generalissimo employs a few such men," said T'sa Yuang-hung. "They are ruthless and resourceful. I shall put the matter another way. There is, I believe, an American slang expression for this. I don't know what it is, but it suggests that such men know where and how to buy anything."

"What do you suppose he was doing?" asked Kirkwal.

"Serving on the staff of Madame Chiang, one lives a somewhat ascetic life.

One must be available every moment. I suspect he decided to break away and find for himself an evening's pleasure. Unhappily for Liang P'ing, he was found by men as evil as he was himself."

"Forgive me if I observe that you don't seem much upset over the death of Liang P'ing," said Kirkwal bluntly.

T'sa Yuang-hung shrugged. "He was, of course, not of my social class."

Major Henry S. Hooker was an old, old friend, a family friend who had been close to the Roosevelts since before the First World War. The President's cocktail hour today would be special for him, because Harry Hooker would join him.

Because Harry would be there, the First Lady broke her usual rule of avoiding the cocktail-hour gatherings. Because he wanted Harry to meet her, the President had sent word to Madame Chiang that she and her entourage were welcome in the West Sitting Hall at six o'clock for a strictly informal gathering at which no protocol would be observed and nothing was excluded from conversation.

So it was that when Ike Hoover rolled the cocktail table off the elevator and situated it where the President would want it, Harry Hooker and Mrs. Roosevelt were sitting and chatting with Madame Chiang, while Weng Guo-fang, T'sa Yuang-hung, and Mr. and Miss Kung sat apart and listened.

The full names of Mr. and Miss Kung were never mentioned. Mrs. Roosevelt was reluctant to ask and wondered if there were not something embarrassing about the names. She thought she had heard Madame Chiang once refer to "Kung Ling-peng" when she was speaking Chinese to Weng Guo-fang, but whether or not that was the name of one of the young couple, and if so which, she could not decide. In English, everyone simply spoke of Mr. Kung and Miss Kung, and that was it.

Miss Kung was again dressed in a well-tailored dark-blue suit, with a white shirt and necktie. Harry Hooker stared at her more than he should have, but his stare was only curious, certainly not disapproving, and if Miss Kung noticed it she showed no sign.

A buzzer sounded. The rumble of the

elevator followed. After a moment, President Roosevelt wheeled himself into the room. He was in an ebullient mood.

"The Germans are taking another beating," he said as he maneuvered his wheelchair up to the cocktail table and scanned the bottles and glasses with obvious satisfaction. "If you understand the mind of Hitler, you know why. Having taken a terrible beating at Stalingrad, he had to make a stab somewhere else—either that or admit he'd been beaten. So he sends Manstein into the Caucasus, at the head of a little army not big enough to change the course of the war. Manstein did all right for a while. But tonight he's been stopped. And he'll stay stopped, what you want to bet? If Hitler had a grain of sense, he'd back away and re-form his troops, get ready to oppose a Russian offensive. But that's not the way the man's mind works. He's trying another offensive, and it looks like he's going to lose another army."

"That's great, Frank!" said Harry Hooker, his open, honest face dominated by a great, innocent smile. His reaction was just what the President hoped for and needed. "Got 'em by the short hairs, don't we? Don't we, Frank?"

The President grinned. "Couldn't express it better myself. Now, then . . . How many for the specialty of the house? Roosevelt martinis. Seven-to-one. Guaranteed to lift the spirits!"

"I imagine," said Mrs. Roosevelt, "that Madame Chiang would prefer to join me in a small glass of sherry."

"I learned to appreciate martinis when they were mixed three to one, Mr. President," said Madame Chiang. "I will try one of yours."

"As will I," said Weng Guo-fang solemnly.

The President shook martinis happily, with enthusiasm. He had to shake two mixers to accommodate all who elected to drink them—besides himself, the entire Chinese party and Harry Hooker.

When all were poured and Mrs. Roosevelt had her glass of sherry, the President lifted his glass. "To the continuing friendship between our two great nations," he said.

They sipped, and Madame Chiang responded. "Also," she said, "to the warm personal friendship that has developed during the week we have enjoyed such kind hospitality."

The First Lady watched the Chinese react to her husband's favorite cocktail. Madame Chiang was not surprised and sipped with a certain bemused curiosity. T'sa Yuang-hung had made the mistake of taking a great swallow with the first toast, and he was trying to be inconspicuous about his discomfort. Weng Guo-fang showed no sign whatever that he found his martini pleasant or unpleasant. The two Kungs had sipped charily and were only a little distressed by the volatile mixture of gin and vermouth.

Shortly the President was cheerfully shaking again. His guests enjoyed his concoction.

Miss Kung, when she had finished her first martini and accepted her second, stepped to the side of Harry Hooker as he, too, was holding out his stem glass to receive a second drink from the spout of the President's shaker. "Have you ever visited China, Mr. Hooker?" she asked.

"I'm afraid not," he said. "I should like to." He glanced at Mrs. Roosevelt, who was standing beside Miss Kung. "I know Eleanor would like to, also."

"You must," said Miss Kung. "You might gain a very different impression of our country."

"Yes. I expect I would."

"We have a rich tradition," the young woman went on. "I myself am a direct lineal descendant, in the seventy-fifth generation, from K'ung-Fu-tzu, whom you know in the West as Confucius."

Hooker turned to the First Lady. "Eleanor," he said, "I didn't know China had a Newport set."

Mrs. Roosevelt could not hold back her laughter.

Miss Kung obviously did not understand the allusion and fortunately was not offended. "Yes," she said. "China has a long and rich tradition of scholarly thought, philosophy, art, and literature—most of which, I am afraid, is little known in the West."

Harry Hooker looked down into the solemn face of the little Chinese woman and realized she was making an earnest plea. He nodded, meaning she should understand he was listening. "We have, for example, at Harvard University, a school of Chinese studies, entirely devoted to Chinese history and culture," he said. "There are other such schools. We may appreciate you more than you realize, Miss Kung."

"I am glad to hear it," she said. "To many Chinese, it seems that Americans suppose we are all laundrymen."

"Oh, my dear!" Mrs. Roosevelt laughed. "We don't think that."

"I am glad to hear it," said Miss Kung gravely.

"We are glad that China has so enthusiastically welcomed Christian missionaries," said Hooker. "We are glad so many Chinese have embraced the Christian faith."

Miss Kung shook her head. "Very few have done that," she said. "Very few." She glanced across the room to Madame Chiang, who was chatting with the President. "Her family embraced Christianity. But very few Chinese, really, have surrendered our ancient traditions and philosophy to take up an alien religion."

"Our missionaries return with stories of entire villages converting," said Hooker.

"Your missionaries brought food and

medicine," said Miss Kung. "As long as they were in the village with those benefits, so long were there Christians. And when they left, there were none."

"We are encouraged to believe China may become a Christian nation," said Hooker.

Miss Kung shook her head. "You are told wrong," she said.

Mrs. Roosevelt decided this conversation had reached an end, so she smiled and murmured that she should speak with Madame Chiang and the President.

"Well, it's interesting to hear your opinion, Miss Kung," said Hooker lamely.

Miss Kung smiled for the first time and sipped gin. "I could be wrong," she said. "It is usually foolish to attempt to predict the future."

Madame Chiang was sitting near the President's wheelchair. Weng Guo-fang sat beside her, dressed this evening in gray suit. Mr. Kung and T'sa Yuang-hung stood behind the President, listening respectfully. Mrs. Roosevelt came and stood beside Madame Chiang.

"I am . . . puzzled by something, Mr. President," said Weng Guo-fang. He had finished his second martini and reached to put the glass aside on the cocktail table. "I find it difficult to understand how some of your workers can be allowed to threaten strikes, at the very time when your nation is committed to a desperate effort to survive a major war."

"I find it difficult myself," said the President.

"The way this man John L. Lewis speaks of you," said Madame Chiang, shaking her head. "His words are not just disrespectful; they are vile. I do not understand how you can tolerate such a thing."

"Well . . . Just what would you do about him, Madame Chiang?"

She smiled faintly, then lifted her hand, placed one of her rapier-long fingernails on her throat, and slowly drew it across, ear to ear.

Half an hour later, all had left the West Sitting Hall except Harry Hooker, Mrs. Roosevelt, and the President. The President put his finger to his throat and drew it across, mimicking the gesture Madame Chiang had made.

"Well, Babs," he said. "Where's your sweet, gentle character now?"

X

Captain Ed Kennelly stood with his hands on his hips, staring down at the silent corpse lying face down in a black puddle in a cinder-paved alley. It was the body of a woman. Since she had fallen there the water in the puddle had frozen, and a thin layer of ice had formed around her ears.

Sergeant Gene Hupp squatted beside her. "Here's what I figured would interest you, Captain," he said. "We opened her purse, looking for identification, before we so much as rolled her over; and here's what we found."

He reached into the purse with a hand swathed in a white handkerchief. He pulled out a tiny glass vial. He stood and displayed the bottle in the handkerchief.

"Little red pills," he said. "What you said we should be on the lookout for. Little red pills."

Kennelly looked at the woman. "Who she?"

"Alias Barbara Lowe," he said. "God knows what her right name is. Alias Bobby Banks. Alias Patricia Harlowe. Alias . . . Street hooker. Got an arrest record that covers two single-spaced sheets."

"What killed her?"

"Good question."

For the second time in two days, Kennelly found himself in Dr. Englander's autopsy lab.

"Not a mark on her," said Dr. Englander. "Don't think she died of natural causes, do you?"

Kennelly stared at yet another naked corpse, this one of a used-up looking woman of maybe forty years—probably younger, but with a body so thoroughly abused that it lied about its age. The expression on the face was distressing. She looked as if she had welcomed death, maybe as a release. He could see she had been pretty, once. Her long dark hair was still pretty. Her face had been pretty. It was ravaged: ruddy and puffy, with flaccid muscles; and the corners of her mouth turned down. Still, Kennelly could see she had been seductive in her way.

"I haven't cut her," said Dr. Englander. "Like you asked. I drew some blood."

"I'm looking for a telephone call," said Kennelly.

"So'm I. I sent the blood to the lab."

"I sent her pills to the lab."

"What kind of pills?"

"That's what I want to know. I kept out a couple to look at." Kennelly took a small tin box from his jacket pocket. "Look at those, Doc. Ever see anything like them?"

Dr. Englander opened the box and frowned over two small tablets, dull-red in color. He shook his head. "Well, they ain't Carter's Little Liver Pills," he said.

Kennelly took out his pack and lit a Lucky. The doctor accepted his offer and lit one, too. The smoke partially overcame the cold, medicinal smell of the laboratory where in a few minutes another human body would be sliced open and its organs examined. Autopsy, Kennelly thought, was the ultimate intrusion. He did not recognize the irony in his idea.

The telephone rang. The call was for Dr. Englander. He listened for a moment, thanked his caller, and turned to Kennelly. "Her blood is full of an alkaloid of opium. Could be morphine or heroin. Maybe both."

"What I figured," said Kennelly.

He walked over and looked down at the body. "Barbara, I wish you could tell me where you got the pills," he said. "I guess you didn't have any experience with them. You should have been more careful."

The doctor gave the cold corpse an almost-affectionate slap on its bare hip. "I doubt very much that this one was ever careful about anything. At least not for a long time. She was drinking, too. Her blood is also laced with alcohol. What a deadly combination! No wonder she passed out."

"Anything for a thrill?"

Dr. Englander stared at her face for a moment. "I expect so. Anything to relieve the sordidness of her life. Look at the bruises on her legs. Some guy—probably more than one guy—gave her rough sex within the past few days. You see bruises like that on a rape victim."

The phone rang again. The call was for Kennelly.

"Okay," he said to Dr. Englander. "The little red pills are heroin. The tablets are crudely made and don't all contain the same amount of the drug. But the ones the lab examined average about two hundred milligrams—"

"Two or three pills would have been enough to kill her," said Dr. Englander. "With the alcohol."

"We haven't seen these pills in the District before," said Kennelly. "Anyway, I haven't."

"I haven't either," said the doctor. "We're not unfamiliar with drugs in the District, but I've never seen the like of this."

"I've got a damned good suspicion where they came from," said Kennelly grimly. "A *damned* good suspicion."

For another long moment he stared at the corpse of Barbara Lowe. "Say, Doc. Your autopsy report on George Shen said he'd taken some codeine or morphine. Could that have been heroin, by any chance?"

The doctor scratched his cheek for a moment. "The lab report said an alkaloid of opium, now that I think of it. Yeah, that could have meant heroin."

"Plus alcohol," said Kennelly. "But he lived to break into the White House and get himself murdered."

"A time factor," said Dr. Englander. "I'd guess Shen gulped his pill—probably only one—hours before he came to the White House. If he was addicted, that would have been his daily lift. Then maybe he enhanced his courage with a drink or three, just before he did whatever he did."

"It is your theory, then," said Mrs. Roosevelt, "that Mr. Liang P'ing somehow carried a large quantity of these pills from China and somehow smuggled them out of the White House and sold them."

"Think about it," said Kennelly. "No one examined the contents of the luggage carried by Madame Chiang and her party. Right?"

"That is correct."

"And there is a lot of it?"

The First Lady nodded. "A very large quantity, I should say. Trunks, bags. Even some wooden crates."

"So, Liang P'ing, who was a crook from the word go, included a fortune's worth of these red pills in the Chiang luggage. I think you said he was in charge of luggage."

"He was the factotum," said Kirkwal. "He was in charge of what we might call logistics."

"When Liang P'ing left the White House, was he carrying a suitcase, or any other container?" asked Mrs. Roosevelt.

"I'll check on that," said Kirkwal. "No record is kept, but the guard may remember."

"The question is," said Kennelly, "can we search the Chinese luggage?"

Mrs. Roosevelt shook her head dubiously. "I'm not certain," she said. "I suppose we should ask for Madame Chiang's permission."

"Are we sure she's not part of the scheme?" asked Kennelly. "There could be a lot of money in it. Suppose they dropped pills in New York, too. I'm sorry to have to say this, Ma'am, but the Chiang government doesn't have the world's finest reputation."

"The little red pills are made by the

Japanese," said Kirkwal. "So said Miss Chin. I've checked into that. The Bureau of Narcotics confirms what she says. The Japanese are cultivating opium and manufacturing the pills. They are a crude alkaloid of opium, squeezed into crude tablets. Some of the more knowledgeable users dissolve them in distilled water and inject them with needles. Most of them are simply swallowed. They are deadly. Hundreds of people have died from swallowing them. Most people who take them become addicted. The pills come from many factories, and their content varies. Some of them are adulterated. A few are just chalk. Some are an opium alkaloid mixed with strychnine or arsenic."

"Are many of them being imported into the United States?" asked Mrs. Roosevelt.

"The Bureau of Narcotics," said Kirkwal, "reports that they show up in considerable numbers on the West Coast. A great many have been seized in Hawaii."

They were sitting in Mrs. Roosevelt's study, and she rose from her desk and went to the window, where she looked out across the Ellipse. A light snow had begun to fall, swirling on the wind. She couldn't see as far as the Tidal Basin.

"The difficulty with all this," she said, "is that it is distracting us from our chief problem, which is the death of Mr. Shen. We must find out—we simply *must* find out—more about that murder. We must learn the significance of the coded message and the map."

"They are all interrelated, I imagine," said Kirkwal. "Maybe I'm wrong, but I suspect it all ties together somehow."

"What have you done with Chin Yulin?" Kennelly asked.

The Chinese girl was lodged in a pair of rooms on the third floor of the White House. She was allowed to wander through the house and look at everything. Mrs. Roosevelt had asked one of the presidential secretaries to eat lunch and dinner with her, so she wouldn't be alone all the time. Even so, she had told the secretary last evening that she was bored and wondered if she was allowed to leave the White House and have a look at the city. The secretary checked. Miss Chin was not in custody. She was free to leave the White House any time she wished.

She had wished this morning, Thursday. When Mrs. Roosevelt was looking thoughtfully out the window at the snow, Chin Yu-lin was on Pennsylvania Avenue, walking toward the Capitol.

Word that she had left the White House had been sent from the guard station at the gate to the Secret Service office. Kirkwal knew she had gone out and decided to take the opportunity to search her rooms. He didn't ask Mrs. Roosevelt's permission. He didn't tell Kennelly. He simply went up to the third floor and used his master key to enter the bedroom with bath that had been assigned to Chin Yu-lin.

His search was a disappointment. She seemed to have brought with her nothing that might not be expected in the luggage of a nineteen-year-old girl.

Except maybe one thing. She was carrying a letter from George Shen. It read—

Darling,
I've been to Washington, Philadelphia, and New York. I think I can be home by the 26th. Have sold orders

totalling $5421. Have a promise for another big order, $825 worth.

Be sure to show this letter to Ben. He'll want to know the numbers.

I am counting the hours and even the minutes till we are together again.

Your faithful lover,
George

Kirkwal picked up the telephone and asked the switchboard to ring the Secret Service office. When an agent answered, he said, "Jack? Come up to Room 324 toot-dee-sweet. Bring along a camera. I've got a document I want photographed."

While he waited for the agent to arrive, he telephoned the gatehouse and left orders that he was to be notified if Chin Yu-lin returned. Also, he asked whether or not the rest of the Chinese party was in the White House or had gone out. The word was that Madame Chiang, with Mr. and Miss Kung, had left by limousine for a luncheon at the Army-Navy Club. Weng Guo-fang had left earlier, as had T'sa Yuang-hung. Only the two maids were in the White House.

Jack Carmichael arrived, carrying a

Leica 35mm camera. Kirkwal smoothed the letter out under a gooseneck lamp on the small desk opposite the window, and Carmichael photographed it.

"Look, Jack. While I've got a chance, I'm gonna search 306 and maybe 326, too. You guard the stairs. The two maids are in Madame Chiang's suite downstairs. If one of them tries to come up, you block the stairs and don't let her up here. Okay? I'll take the camera."

Jack Carmichael nodded. He stationed himself in the east stair hall.

Room 306 was assigned to T'sa Yuang-hung. Kirkwal found a certain military precision in the way he ordered his possessions: twin hair brushes in a precise line on his dresser top, bottles of hair tonic, shaving lotion, and cologne in another carefully laid line. His clothes were sorted and hung in his closet—jackets together, then trousers, then shirts.

If he owned anything that was revealing, he had hidden it well. Kirkwal went through his pockets, felt the linings of his jackets and waistbands, searched through his drawers, even through his laundry— and found nothing.

Kirkwal knew what Kennelly would say. This orderliness was so complete as to be suspicious.

Room 326 had been Liang P'ing's. What Kirkwal found there was no evidence; but it was suggestive. In this room, too, everything was arranged with determined neatness.

Was it possible the Shanghai pimp and ex-convict had kept his room this way? No. At least it was extremely unlikely. Kirkwal guessed that T'sa Yuang-hung had spent an hour or more in this room.

Why would he bother? Why would T'sa Yuan-hung trouble himself to arrange so methodically the possessions of a man he had despised?

"Because he conducted a thorough search of Mr. Liang's room," said Mrs. Roosevelt.

"T'sa Yuang-hung is a Kuomintang security officer," said Captain David Bloom, the navy cryptanalyst and intelligence officer. "That would be his business, to search the room of a member of the party who was murdered."

"What I'd like to know," said Ed Kennelly, "is whether he removed any evidence."

"If there was any evidence there, he removed it," said Bobby Kirkwal.

"That would be his duty," said Bloom.

"Whether or not it was his duty, I should think, depends on what kind of evidence he removed," said Mrs. Roosevelt.

"Pills . . ." said Kirkwal.

"Coded messages, and maps," said Mrs. Roosevelt.

"Which," said Captain Bloom, "brings us to your reason for asking me to meet with you."

They were meeting in the Cabinet Room, in the thought that the President might want to join them if anything worth his attention developed. He had expressed continuing concern about the encoded message found on the body of George Shen.

"Does the letter found in Miss Chin's room mean anything?" asked Mrs. Roosevelt.

"Possibly," said Captain Bloom. "You notice that Shen mentioned three cities, again in reverse alphabetical order—an order that in the context doesn't seem to make much sense. Then he mentions two numbers, 5421 and 825. When we reverse those, they are 1245 and 528. We have no idea what those numbers might mean, either straight or reversed. Significantly, however, the numbers 1245 and 528 have occurred two or three times recently in Japanese naval radio traffic."

"It cannot be a coincidence," said Mrs. Roosevelt soberly. "I mean, mathematically . . ."

"That is true," said Captain Bloom.

"We are therefore almost unquestionably confronted with an espionage plot," she said. "And we simply must focus all our attention on that element of our mystery."

"Shen and Chin," said Kennelly.

"What?"

"George Shen and Chin Yu-lin are the only people we can definitely identify as having any connection with the coded messages," said Kennelly. "I figure there's a connection between them and the little red pills, but so far we haven't made any connection."

"Except that George Shen was taking the little red pills," said Kirkwal.

"And talking about coincidences," said Kennelly. "Isn't it just a little too much of a coincidence that Barbara Lowe dies of swallowing little red pills just one day after Liang P'ing disappears and is murdered?"

"*Still,*" insisted Mrs. Roosevelt, "we have established no relationship between the pills and espionage."

"To what extent are the pills a problem in San Francisco?" asked Kirkwal. "Maybe you should telephone your newspaper publisher friend."

"I'll do that right now," said the First Lady.

She picked up a telephone and told the switchboard to put her through to Edward Greschner at the San Francisco Chronicle.

"The Bureau of Narcotics confirms that they are a problem," said Kennelly.

"Did you have a chance to take fingerprints from Miss Chin's letter?" asked Mrs. Roosevelt.

"No," said Kirkwal. The Secret Service doesn't have fingerprinting capability."

"Where are the Chinks now?" asked Kennelly. He didn't notice Mrs. Roosevelt's disapproving frown over his use of the term Chinks. He went on. "Still out?"

"Madame Chiang and the Kungs are back in her suite," said Kirkwal. "Weng Guo-fang came in a short while ago. Chin Yu-lin and T'sa Yuang-hung are still out."

"I should like to know where *she* is," said Mrs. Roosevelt.

"I'll be glad to put her where we'll know where she is when we want her," said Kennelly.

"No . . . I think we shouldn't. We should, though, get her answer to the question of whether or not she did in fact show Mr. Shen's letter to 'Ben.' "

"I'd like to know who 'Ben' is," said Kennelly.

The telephone rang. Mrs. Roosevelt picked it up. It was her call to the publisher Edward Greschner. They exchanged pleasantries, then—

"Ed, have you ever heard of a drug coming into the country, called 'the little red pill'?"

"I've heard of it."

"Is it a problem in San Francisco?"

"Sure. Any drug's a problem. This one seems to be some kind of opium derivative, and the rumor is that the Japs are trying to flood the world with it."

"Suppose I told you George Shen was taking the pill. What would that suggest to you?"

"That another member of our Chinese community has been victimized by another form of opium."

"Ah. A woman died here last night as the result of taking that pill."

"Can I publish that?"

"I should be grateful if you would. The nation should be warned."

"Where did she get it?"

"That we don't know. I can speculate on it but would rather not."

"I meant to call you. I have a little further information on your man Shen. O and O tells me he traveled to Japan from time to time, during the period when he was in their employ. They sent him at company expense several times, as an English-Chinese-Japanese interpreter; but he made several trips on his own, traveling at his own expense, though of course at a fraction of the regular rate. They don't know what he did there, but each time he stayed in Japan a month or so. He told the company he was brushing up on his vocabulary, his commercial terminology. They liked him, incidentally. They thought he was a loyal employee."

"I am grateful for the information."

"I have a sense that you are working on something big, Eleanor. Also, I have a sense that you cannot possibly talk about it."

"I appreciate your understanding," she said. "Let me put someone on the line. This is Captain Edward Kennelly, detective with the District police. He can tell you about the death caused by the pills. *That* you can publish."

"I'm curious about something, Ed," said Bobby Kirkwal as they left the Executive Wing and walked out into a cold, blustery night, on their way to dinner. "I didn't look at the wet clothes your men had spread out to dry. I mean, I didn't look at whatever Liang P'ing had been wearing. Did it include an overcoat?"

Kennelly shook his head. "Suit."

"Cold night," said Kirkwal. "That means he was killed indoors. Whoever killed him didn't see fit to wrap him in his overcoat."

"A corpse doesn't need an overcoat."

"No. But we know he wasn't killed outdoors. Probably not in a car, either."

"Unless he was hustled out of someplace and into a car, to be taken where he was to be killed. Maybe he was conked on the head, dumped in a car, maybe in the trunk, and hauled out into Maryland to be shot."

"Maybe," said Kirkwal.

"What's your special interest in the overcoat?"

Kirkwal paused as he watched Kennelly light a cigarette. "How many little red pills could you carry out of the White House in the lining of a heavy overcoat? Or in special pockets sewn into an overcoat? Suppose you could hide ten pounds of them in there. What are ten pounds of little red pills worth?"

Kennelly grinned. "You're not focusing on what Mrs. R told us to focus on."

"Okay. Does it worry you that Chin Yulin hasn't come back to the White House?"

"Yeah. That worries me. And I wouldn't know where to start if I went out to look for her."

They need not have worried. Chin Yu-lin was a completely independent young woman. She returned to the White House only a quarter of an hour after they left, carrying with her a few small purchases she had made at Sears, Roebuck and at Woolworth. In her room, she sat before a dressing table and stared at herself in the mirror as she applied the new shade of lipstick she had bought.

She was judging the lipstick when she heard a knock on the door. She went to open it.

"Excuse me," said a handsome young man. "My name is T'sa Yuang-hung. I am a member of Madame Chiang's staff. I noticed that you seem to be alone. Would you like to join me for dinner? We can go out. I know a nice place."

The President's cocktail hour that evening was not a time to unwind. It was a grim conference. The President mixed drinks for Admirals Ernest King and Frank Leahy, for General George Marshall, and for Harry Hopkins.

"Somewhere the Japanese reach a point where they are militarily overextended," said General Marshall. "They have armies tied down in China, French Indo-China, the Dutch East Indies, the Philippines—"

"They're not actually tied down in all those places," said Admiral Leahy. He was Chairman of the Joint Chiefs and the President's personal liaison to the service departments. "In some of them the native population welcomed them, so the Japanese need keep only a token force in place."

"I'd think," said the President, "that the defeat they suffered on Guadalcanal put an end to their idea of invading Australia. But they still have major ground and sea forces in the South Pacific. If they decided to shift their focus toward India, that could be a big new threat."

"They've got naval and air units to spare at Rabaul," said Admiral King.

"All right," said the President. "Suppose they withdrew some significant number of ships, sent them to Singapore, then up the Malacca Strait, and into the Bay of Bengal. Where are we then?"

"I don't think they'll invade India," said General Marshall. "They haven't the forces to hold it. On the other hand, they could take Ceylon."

"Having a major Japanese task force in the Indian Ocean would be a serious threat," said Admiral King.

"Then are we not obligated to move ships there to counter them?" asked the President.

"I see no alternative," said Admiral Leahy. "Can the British supply anything?"

"I'll ask the Former Naval Person," said President Roosevelt.

General Marshall shook his head and frowned. "I hope we are not placing too much credence on this single decoded message," he said.

"I agree," said the President. "I'm troubled. Let's decide what force we can send and plan the operation, but let's don't actually move any ships toward the Indian Ocean just yet. There's something about this thing that bothers me."

"The whole deal bothers me," said Admiral King.

"Exactly what element of it bothers you most?" Harry Hopkins asked the President.

The President had begun to light a cigarette and finished before he answered. "I don't like the way we got the information," he said. "We find a dead body in the White House. In a pocket there's a coded message. The message suggests Japanese interest in the Bay of Bengal and the Indian Ocean. Why was this spy—if he was a spy—carrying that? I'm tempted to forget the whole thing."

"It's stupid beyond belief for a spy—if that's what he was—to be carrying an important message like that around in his pocket," said Harry Hopkins.

"They've got endless confidence in the code," said Admiral Leahy. "They don't dream we've cracked it."

"So we presume," said the President. "And we have to act on that assumption. Start sorting it out, gentlemen. See what ships we can spare. Let's be ready to move."

* * *

Mrs. Roosevelt and Madame Chiang, accompanied by the Kungs and Harry Hooker, left the White House at 7:00 P.M. to drive to Constitution Hall, where a benefit performance was being held to raise funds for the USO.

The stars of the show were Alexandra Danilova of the Ballet Russe de Monte Carlo, one of the world's all-time great ballerinas; Paul Robeson, who would play a scene from his acclaimed revival of *Othello;* and Judith Anderson and Maurice Evans, who would play an act from their *Macbeth.*

A cocktail party was being held before the performance, for the honored guests and the most generous of subscribers—at which the performers would appear and would autograph programs.

"I'm a little curious," said Madame Chiang in the car on their way to Constitution Hall. "Isn't this the hall run by the DAR, the hall where they wouldn't let Marian Anderson sing because she is a Negro? Then how is it that Paul Robeson—?"

"My dear," said Mrs. Roosevelt in her sweetest, most melodious voice, "the bosomy *grande dames* of the DAR have been thoroughly debunked. They would open their hall to a performance by a descendant of Benedict Arnold, if one wanted to play the comb and tissue paper in concert there."

The program contained a statement—

We are now in a war to protect a way of life. In our conflict, all races are allied to fight for common ideals. The Negro pilot of the Army Air Corps may fight under the command of Chiang in China; just as soldiers of other races fought with Venice for the protection of Christianity.

Paul Robeson appeared at the cocktail party in his costume: the armor of a Moorish warrior in the service of sixteenth-century Venice.

"I do ask you, Ma'am," he said to Mrs. Roosevelt when they met and stood apart for a moment's conversation, "when the United States will open the Second Front."

"You will perhaps forgive me, Mr. Robeson," she said, "if I observe that there are more than a few rumors that you have committed yourself to the politics of the Second Front."

She was suggesting that Paul Robeson had allied himself—if he had not indeed become a member—of the Communist Party. The party, following the Stalinist line, was demanding that the United States and Britain throw their forces into an invasion of the continent of Europe, now, even if such an invasion was doomed to failure, because only such a sacrifice could save the Soviet Union.

For a moment the big, strong, black face of Robeson glowered at the First Lady. Then he smiled. "I want to win this war," he said. "I don't see how we can do it if we allow our Soviet comrades to be defeated."

"How can we win it if we throw our resources into a futile effort too soon, before we are ready?" she asked.

He shook his head skeptically.

"Mr. Molotov, when he called on us last year, made this point more forcefully than you can, Mr. Robeson. Perhaps you should rely on him to act as advocate for the Soviet point of view."

"I speak only for the American point of view."

"I am sure you so intend," she said. "But be careful."

He hesitated, frowning, for a moment. Then he nodded emphatically and said, "I appreciate your words."

"Perhaps you will autograph my program," said Mrs. Roosevelt.

"I will," he said. He wrote—

With respect and gratitude to Mrs. Eleanor Roosevelt, February 25, 1943.
Paul Robeson

She turned to introduce him to Madame Chiang, only to discover that the First Lady of China had walked away and was deep within an admiring circle of formally dressed people across the room.

Alexandra Danilova was a beautiful and marvelously talented ballerina who was a very different-looking young woman and yet reminded Mrs. Roosevelt of the petite Nina Rozanov, who had been suspected in the murder of Boris Troyanoski on the *Normandie* five years ago.

The First Lady had met Judith Anderson and Maurice Evans before. They joined her and the ballerina for a few words and to autograph her program before they went backstage to be made up for their appearance as Macbeth and Lady Macbeth.

Because Madame Chiang Kai-shek had retreated from the presence of Paul Robeson, she did not meet these people. Mrs. Roosevelt preferred to believe that Madame's abrupt separation from her was because she thought Robeson was a Communist, not because he was a Negro. It was one of those things of which she could not be sure.

XI

"This is amazing!" T'sa Yuang-hung said to Chin Yu-lin. "Right here, in the American executive mansion!"

"Yes," she said. "George Shen was murdered in the White House."

"Last Wednesday."

"Yes. Last Wednesday evening."

T'sa Yuang-hung shook his head and smiled wonderingly. "Their security must be dangerously loose, to have allowed this to happen within the White House. It is marvelously tight, though, in another respect."

"Watcha mean?"

"We have lived here all this time, and none of us so much as imagined such a thing had happened."

Chin Yu-lin shrugged. "They didn't want you to know."

"I am in charge of protection for Madame Chiang," said T'sa Yuang-hung. "Of course, they don't know that . . . And you won't tell them, will you, Chin Yu-lin?"

They had eaten a fine dinner and had shared a bottle of wine—something not easy to do in wartime Washington. Back in the White House, he had called the pantry and asked for a bottle of whiskey with ice and soda. Now he and Chin Yu-lin were together in his bed, sipping whiskey and smoking. They had made love before they called for the whiskey, and they expected they would again, at least once more tonight.

T'sa Yuang-hung kissed her. "Yu-lin . . ." he whispered.

"Call me Betty," she said.

"Don't you care about anything Chinese?"

She shook her head. "I am an American."

"I am Chinese," he said: a simple, earnest affirmation.

She dragged smoke from her cigarette. "You have a wife at home, don't you? And children."

"As a matter of fact, I do, yes."

"And a smothering Chinese family," she said, a measured scorn in her voice. "Ancestors. All that."

"Yes."

"Where is your home?"

"Peking."

"Ah— Then . . . the Japanese . . ."

He nodded.

"My God, your wife and children?"

T'sa Yuang-hung nodded again.

"Are they alive?" she asked softly.

"I receive letters."

She put her arms around him. "I'm sorry," she muttered into his chest. "I am very sorry."

Fuzzy Cairns was stark naked. His hands were cuffed behind his back, and he was bound to a heavy wooden chair by a length of rope that circled his middle and the back of the chair.

"C'mon, Fuzz," sneered Kennelly. "You been sweated before. Don't get your dander up."

"Never like this," muttered Cairns between swollen lips.

Cairns was a thickset man, maybe forty-five years old—old enough not to have been drafted, in any case—and he sat slumped forward, staring at his naked legs, drawing deep breaths one after another. He had been slapped hard, not really beaten, and his slicked-down hair remained smoothly in place.

"I gotta make water," he mumbled.

"Go ahead," said Kennelly. "Be my guest."

They were alone in a cellar room with brick walls and a concrete floor, and there was a drain in the floor. A rubber hose hung coiled around a faucet. Cairns glanced at it, then glanced at it again. He knew what it was for.

"Kennelly, I don't know what the hell this is all about!"

"Sure ya do. And you're scared shitless. I would be, too, if I was you. You're lookin' at a long, long sentence, Fuzz. Years and years. Everything you got goin' for you will be taken over before you get out. You'll do hard time and a lot of it, and when you get out you'll be a bum."

"Fer what?"

"For sellin' pills without a prescription. Practicin' medicine without a license."

"Ain't nothin' much in them pills," Cairns muttered.

"Oh, no? Okay. That's your ticket outa

trouble, Fuzz. Jeez, it's gonna be easy." Kennelly reached into his jacket pocket and pulled out four of the little red pills. "All you have to do is just swallow these four little pills, which ain't got nothing much in 'em, and you'll prove your case. Here we go. Open your mouth, Fuzz, and I'll poke in the first one."

Fuzzy Cairns's control failed, and his urine ran.

Kennelly grinned. "It's okay, Fuzz. I'll rinse you off."

"No . . ."

Kennelly pulled the coil of hose off the faucet and twisted the handle to turn on the water. He stood back far enough not to be splashed and shot the thick, powerful stream of water on the naked man. He let it run for a minute or so, playing the stream on the man's head, then his back, then his belly and legs. He turned the water off and dropped the hose.

Cairns shuddered and shook his head. The oiled hair now stood up in spikes.

"I got one corpse in the morgue as a result of those pills," said Kennelly. "I want two things from you, and I'm keeping you right here and working on you until you tell me. I want to know where you got those pills, and I want to know who you sold them to. It ain't very nice to work a man this way, and I don't like it. But I'll do it. When we stop is up to you, Fuzz."

Daniel "Fuzzy" Cairns had lived off the main chance for twenty years to Kennelly's certain knowledge. On the record, he had sold moonshine during Prohibition, had run a string of girls as a pimp, had run a score of floating crap games, had sold numbers and football and baseball cards, and was a fence for stolen merchandise. By suspicion, he had sold reefer cigarettes, had been a legbreaker collector for bookies, had transported stolen cars in and out of the District, and maybe, just maybe, had killed one man. He had served six sentences since Kennelly first noticed him—none of them more than ninety days.

"You're a hard man, Kennelly," said Fuzzy Cairns. He was shivering now, from the cold water. "I didn't know those pills—"

"Then why don't you take some?"

"Kennelly! Four of 'em! Hell, man, four of *anything!*"

"Oh . . . Well, take one. Let's see what one will do." The big Irish cop pushed a pill between Cairns's lips. "Just swallow one, Fuzz."

Cairns screamed and spit the pill across the room.

"Hey, Fuzz. You know how they get pills down a horse? Or a dog? Put a little tube in their mouth, shove it down their throat, then put the pill in the tube and . . . *poof!* Blow. And the pill goes down. Now, man, you couldn't really object, could you, if I asked you to take one or two of the pills you were selling?"

"Kennelly . . ." The man began to sob. "Hey, Kennelly!"

"Ready to talk? Or— Want another shower bath, or some pills, or what?"

Fuzzy Cairns drew a deep breath and let it go with a shudder. "What do I get if I talk?"

"You get to walk to your cell. You get to lie down on a nice warm cot and go to sleep. I mean, you can go to sleep and figure you're gonna wake up, 'cause you haven't swallowed any of your own pills. You're gonna have room and board for a while. *Quite* a while, probably. Warm and dry."

Cairns blew a loud breath: sigh or

sob, one or the other. "Someday you're gonna get yours, too, Kennelly," he muttered.

"We'll worry about that later. Right now, I want to know where you got the little red pills."

"You ain't gonna like the answer."

"I'd better like it."

"You ain't gonna like it, 'cause I don't know who sold 'em to me. And that's the goddamn truth!"

Kennelly picked up the hose. "Fuzz, I got a corpse in the morgue. Let's go at this another way. How many pills did you buy?"

"Fifty."

"What'd you pay for 'em?"

"Two hunnert bucks."

"What'd you sell 'em for?"

"Some eight bucks, some ten bucks apiece."

"Yeah. Harmless little pills. Got nothin' in 'em. *Fuzz . . .*"

"How's I to know somebody'd take too many all at once?"

"I want to know who you sold them to."

"How do I know? Do I know the name of every doper on the streets?"

"You know the name Barbara Lowe? Bobby Banks? Patricia Harlowe?"

"No. I don't know any of them girls."

Kennelly opened the valve and shot the powerful stream of cold water on Cairns. He walked around him, hitting him in the face as the man tried to duck away, hitting him on the belly, on his genitals, until Fuzzy Cairns yelled—

"Stop! I know her!"

"Which one?"

"They're all the same."

"You sell her any pills?"

"She bought three."

"She's dead, Fuzz. That's who I've got in the morgue. And that puts you away for life. The only chance you've got for anything less is to help me get my hands on your wholesaler."

"Which I'd do," Cairns sobbed. He shuddered. "Which I'd do. But I swear to you I don't know the guy. He knew 'bout me. He came to me. I couldn't find him again, no way. He said he'd look me up in a week or so and see if I needed any more merchandise. I swear that's true, Kennelly. I swear to God that's true!"

"Describe the guy."

"A Chink. An old Chink. Who'd ya figure but a Chink?"

Pearl Buck, who was visiting Washington and staying at the Madison Hotel, had telephoned Mrs. Roosevelt to express her regret in having to decline an invitation to come to the White House.

"I should like to have an opportunity to explain, in a bit more detail than I can in a phone conversation," she had said.

The First Lady had suggested they meet for breakfast or lunch. They met for breakfast on Friday morning, at the Madison.

They sat down in the breakfast room. It was in the nature of the hotel and its usual clientele that no one would disturb the famous pair in the privacy of their breakfast. So they sat at a corner table. Jack Carmichael of the Secret Service sat at the next table.

"I hope I was not abrupt or rude in declining your kind invitation to dinner with Madame Chiang," said Pearl Buck.

"I didn't take it so at all," said Mrs. Roosevelt.

"To hear the woman talk about 'democracy' simply sticks in my craw. She and her husband are anything but democratic. She is a member of the Chinese aristocracy, if there is such a thing. She is a member of the wealthy and ruling class, anyway. He was born a peasant and clawed his way to power. He is a warlord. He is simply another of the Chinese warlords. Democracy has no chance in China under the regime of the Chiangs."

"I understand," said Mrs. Roosevelt. "She is an interesting woman, and I can't help but feel friendly toward her. Yet—"

"Do you remember what I warned you about at the beginning of the war?" asked Pearl Buck. "About race?"

"I remember vividly. You told me that the Japanese would be welcomed in many parts of Asia, because many Asian peoples would regard the war as a war against the white man."

"Yes. And I said something had to be done about Negro inequality in the United States. How can we ask Negro men to fight for this country when we tolerate—? Well, we tolerate *lynching.*"

"I would not say we tolerate it," said Mrs. Roosevelt. "We just haven't managed to abolish it."

"Well, your friend Madame Chiang has identified herself rather completely with the opponents of racial equality in this country."

"Madame Chiang has but one interest and courts whomever she thinks can help her promote it. That interest is increased assistance to China."

"Her forthcoming tour of the States is controlled by people who scorn the Negro race, scorn Asians—and, for that matter, scorn the President and scorn you."

"I am afraid I have to acknowledge there is an element of truth in that," said Mrs. Roosevelt. "I've had a distressing experience. Walter White, of the NAACP, invited Madame Chiang to address a meeting of the NAACP. She would be given the opportunity to explain the Chinese cause to thousands of Negroes."

"She declined, I imagine," said Pearl Buck.

Mrs. Roosevelt nodded. "Even though

I was to appear on the platform with her—which I would have done with my husband's approval—she refused, saying she would appear only at meetings sponsored by her 'friends.' "

"Meaning the friends of Henry Luce," said Pearl Buck.

"What is worse, she refused even to see Walter White, even to talk to him, privately."

"This is why I will not come to the White House while she is there. This and other reasons."

"Well . . . She's leaving Sunday."

"Very carefully," said Bobby Kirkwal to Jack Carmichael.

Carmichael had returned to the White House after Mrs. Roosevelt's breakfast and was hearing his new assignment.

"I don't even know if you can do it, Jack. But do it carefully, subtly."

"Understood," said Carmichael.

It was not an easy assignment. Jack Carmichael was to attempt to take pictures of Weng Guo-fang and T'sa Yuang-hung without their knowing it. He would have to conceal what he was doing from his subjects, within the White House. What was more, the assignment was technologically difficult. Obviously, he would have to use existing light. Also he would have to use a telephoto lens. The combination challenged the limits of the speed of any film available to him.

Carmichael was a skilled photographer, though. He was an avid amateur, and he had brought his talent to the Secret Service, which often wanted pictures of people who approached the President in crowds, for later identification.

He affixed a 135mm lens to the Leica, and he used Agfa Superpan Press film. That was the best he could do.

T'sa Yuang-hung proved to be less of a problem than he had expected. He strolled out of the White House in mid-morning, on his way to the north gate; and Carmichael, readied by a call from the House, stationed himself by the fence and near the gatehouse and shot pictures with no trouble.

Weng Guo-fang was more difficult. He remained in his room most of the morning, then moved only as far as Madame Chiang's suite.

It was necessary to ask Mrs. Roosevelt to cooperate in luring him into the light.

She telephoned him. "Mr. Weng," she said. "I wonder if I could ask a favor of you?"

"Any favor I can perform, honored lady."

"We have on a table in the Green Room a lovely piece of Chinese porcelain. It is a monteith, I believe. I wonder if you would come and take a look at it and tell me if you can identify it."

Ten minutes later they were in the Green Room, and Carmichael was there with his Leica, with normal lens now mounted.

The piece, sitting on a table, was a deep oblong bowl with a high, scalloped rim, decorated with painted carnations, poppies, and zinnias.

"We think it came to the White House during the presidency of James Monroe," said Mrs. Roosevelt. "It seems to have been used as a punch bowl."

"If so used, correctly used," said Weng Guo-fang. "Also, sometimes chipped ice was put in, and then wineglasses, to cool them."

"Is it old? Is it rare?"

"Pieces like this," said Weng Guo-fang, "were produced in China for export to Europe." He nodded. "Trade goods, as you might say."

"Then nothing distinguished?"

"Oh, to the contrary. Few of these survive. They are rare and valuable. This dates from the Ch'ing Dynasty, K'ang-hsi period. Between 1662 and 1722. The designers and craftsmen who made these had no idea what a punchbowl was used for, so the item makes a far from ideal punchbowl."

"How very interesting. Would you mind if we photographed you with it? Would you hold it and be photographed with it? That would make a wonderful souvenir of your visit."

Weng Guo-fang smiled and nodded, and Jack Carmichael took several pictures, with flash.

"Gone for about six hours," said Kirkwal to Mrs. Roosevelt. "We've got no idea where she was. But we know where she went. She went out to dinner with T'sa Yuang-hung, and when they came back she went to bed with him."

"Love at first sight," said Kennelly dryly.

"It suggests they knew each other before," said the First Lady.

"It suggests to me that the girl has no morals," said Kennelly.

"That may be a given," said Mrs. Roosevelt. "The question is, did they know each other before—and if so, what is the significance of that?"

"I think the time has come to sweat her," said Kennelly.

"I suppose you mean rigorous interrogation. How can you justify it?"

"Two ways," Kirkwal interjected. "The President may be about to shift a naval task force from somewhere in the South Pacific, where we know it is desperately needed, to somewhere in the Indian Ocean, where it may be needed only if that coded message is valid. How many lives are put at risk if that movement is unnecessary?"

"I'll give you the second reason," said

Kennelly. "One woman is dead because of the little red pills—"

"But that may have nothing to do with—"

"Chin Yu-lin says she found seventeen little red pills in Shen's room in San Francisco."

Mrs. Roosevelt glanced at her watch. She had a luncheon appointment. "What do you propose to do to her?" she asked.

"Make her afraid," said Kennelly. "Nothing more."

The First Lady shook her head. "So much at stake . . . So many lives . . ."

"We won't hurt her," said Kennelly firmly.

"Mr. Kirkwal, I hold you responsible for that. It's not that I don't trust Captain Kennelly, but you are a federal officer, and—"

"Just a little learning experience," said Kennelly. "Bobby can cut it off with a word, any time."

"I am reluctant about this. But too much is at stake."

* * *

Kennelly faced Fuzzy Cairns, through the heavy steel bars of a cell in the District jail.

"You gave me pneumonia, Kennelly," said Cairns hoarsely.

"They've got a good hospital at Leavenworth," said Kennelly. "Good one at Atlanta, too. 'Course, maybe— You may qualify for Alcatraz, Fuzz. Record like yours. Woman dead from what you sold her."

"I got the shakes," Cairns whispered. "I got a fever."

"I can cool you off."

"Oh, God no! You'd kill me!"

"Could be. I don't give a damn about that, Fuzz. You gave my steno a list of the people you sold pills to. Only one more name. We got to the guy in time. You got one murder charge against you. Just one. Maybe you'll think of some more names, so we can get to others in time. But that's neither here nor there. My big problem is, where did you get the pills?"

Cairns leaned against the bars, pressing his forehead between two of them, marking it with red lines. "Kennelly . . ."

"I want you to look at some pictures, Fuzz. Two pictures. 'Kay? Here."

He handed Cairns the pictures of Weng Guo-fang and T'sa Yuang-hung. "Ever see those Chinks?"

Fuzzy Cairns looked at the photographs Jack Carmichael had taken.

"Hey . . . Which one you want me to say I've seen?"

Kennelly shook his head. "Only the one you've really seen, you damned dummy! Don't send me off on a wild-goose chase, Fuzz."

"Kennelly . . . I ain't never seen one of these Chinks, that I know of. God, they all look alike, but neither one of these guys is the one that sold me the pills. I swear that!"

Kennelly grabbed the pictures from his hand. "Damn!"

He walked away from the cell.

"Kennelly! I helped! C'mon! Say I helped!"

Chin Yu-lin sat in the backseat of the D.C. police car driven by Kennelly. Kirkwal sat in the front beside Kennelly, but he kept turned on his seat, looking at her.

Kennelly had driven up into Rock

Creek Park, and here he pulled the car to the side of the road and stopped.

Bobby Kirkwal asked the questions. He was the handsome one, the one with the handsome square face and cleft chin and the disarming East London accent.

"Yu-lin," he said. "Do you know what's at stake in the possibility that George Shen was a Japanese spy?"

"Why'd you bring me out here?" she asked fearfully.

"Well, we're not going to kill you and dump your body by the side of the road, if that's what you have in mind," said Kirkwal. "But we are not in a position to be entirely gentle in our interrogation."

"I done nothin'."

"Well, where did you sleep last night?"

She shrugged. "In bed. Where you figure?"

"In whose bed?"

"In *my* bed. Where else?"

Kirkwal shook his head. "In T'sa Yuang-hung's bed. Don't be stupid, Yu-lin."

She blew a loud breath. "Nobody's business . . ."

Kennelly nudged Kirkwal and handed him a pair of handcuffs.

"Tell you what, Yu-lin—"

"Call me Betty," she said. "Betty is what I want to be called."

"Good enough. Now, Betty, I'm giving you a pair of handcuffs. I want you to put them on. Put them on yourself. Right now."

"Hey! What for? What the hell . . . ?"

Kennelly spoke. "Maybe you're on your way to jail, Betty. It depends. Put the handcuffs on, so you'll know what they feel like. Get an idea what kind of trouble you're in."

Chin Yu-lin sobbed. "I don't want to put these on, guys! Don't make me!"

"What do you want to tell us, then?" asked Kirkwal.

"Honest to Jesus Christ, guys! I don't know nothin'!"

"How did George Shen come to speak fluent Japanese?" asked Kirkwal.

"I dunno!"

"He wrote you a letter. It's in your room. It's in a Jap code. You were supposed to show it to Ben, who would know what it meant. Who's Ben?"

"The guy he worked for . . ."

"Shoe company," said Kirkwal.

"What he said."

"You meet this Ben?"

"I never met anybody he worked with. He mentioned this Ben just before he left San Francisco, and he said Ben would get in touch with me. But he never did. He wrote that I was supposed to show the letter to Ben, but no Ben never called me, so I couldn't show anything to him."

"So how you figure that?"

"Hey! George was a goddamn crook! Some kind . . . I figured that. *Spy . . .?* God, I swear it never come to my mind!"

"Pills?"

She nodded. "Maybe. He spoke Jap."

"You slept with T'sa Yuang-hung last night. Did you ever meet him before?"

Chin Yu-lin shook her head. Her eyes were fixed on the handcuffs. She gripped them in both hands and stared at them in horror.

"Did he pay you?"

She shook her head. "I'm not that kind of girl," she murmured.

"Are you really not?" asked Kirkwal, his musical lower-middle-class English accent taking over his voice. "He must be quite an appealing fellow, then."

"His family are prisoners of the Japs," she said. "Wife, children, father, mother . . ."

"Did he tell you anything we need to know?" asked Kennelly.

"No. We talked about his family, about his home . . . about mine."

"You haven't put the handcuffs on, Yu-lin," said Kirkwal. "Do that now."

"*Please . . .*"

"Now, Yu-lin."

Her hands trembled, and she sobbed as she put the cuffs around her wrists and shoved the steel tongues into the snapping locks. "Am I under arrest?" she wept.

"Not yet the way it makes a criminal record, if you cooperate," said Kennelly.

"Instead of our asking questions, Yu-lin, I think it would be better if you just told us the story of your meeting with Yuang-hung, in your own words, and however the story comes to you."

The girl slipped the handcuffs back and forth on her wrists. That instantly became a tic; she slipped them back and forth incessantly as she talked. "I went out to look around town yesterday," she said.

"Never seen Washington. I walked all the way up to the Capitol. Then I walked around and did some shopping. Got lost. Had to ask a cop which way to the White House. When I got back and was in my room, Yuang-hung came to the door and asked me to go out to dinner. So we went to dinner. He said he knew a nice restaurant, and he did, too. We went to a place called Harvey's. He pointed out J. Edgar Hoover, of the FBI, who was having dinner across the room with a man called Tolson. He said those two men were a scandal that everybody in Washington knew but no newspaper dared report."

"He's been in Washington before," said Kirkwal.

"I s'pose so. Is that a surprise? He said he's in charge of Madame Chiang's safety."

"Go on."

"He talked about the war. He said China can't win if the United States doesn't send more help. But he said Americans are white people and don't care about what happens to Orientals, any more than they care about their niggers."

"He used that word? 'Niggers?' "

"Yes. He said I ought to think about that, 'cause I'm a nigger, too, in the eyes of many Americans."

"What did you say to that?"

"I laughed at him."

"Go on."

"Well . . . When we were walking up from the gate to the White House, he talked about what an experience it was to be sleeping in the White House. I said it was something I'd remember the rest of my life. Then he asked me if I'd sleep with him. He said he was lonesome."

"He'd told you his wife was a prisoner of the Japanese."

"No. He only told me that after we'd been in bed awhile. Hey. He didn't tell me that to get me to go to bed with him! I mean . . . I believe it. I think the poor guy—"

"What else did he say?"

"Well . . . He knows about George. He said you guys were trying to keep it secret, but— But . . . Damn! Maybe I told the secret! Hey, I didn't mean to! He asked me what I was doing staying in the White House— I mean, he asked me that over dinner. And I told him. Maybe I . . . Oh, Jesus!"

She began to cry.

"Put your hands up here, Miss Chin," said Kennelly. "I'll unlock the cuffs."

XII

Leading events of the Washington year were the semi-annual dinners of the Gridiron Club, the famous and exclusive club for professional journalists. The dinner for December 1941 was canceled; and, except for small, members-only private dinners, no more were held until December 1945. The Gridiron Club was then exclusively a men's club. Women could not become members. Women were not invited to the dinners.

The dinners featured skits, in which no political figure was too high to be lampooned. At a 1940 dinner, a character representing Secretary of the Treasury Henry Morgenthau sang to a character representing President Roosevelt and mocked his failure to balance the budget.

Because women—particularly the wives of the men invited to the Gridiron

Club dinner—could not attend, women held a dinner on the same night, called the Widow's Club dinner. For the Widow's Club dinner of 1938, Mrs. Roosevelt and Mrs. Morgenthau—the First Lady's dear friend Elinor, wife of the Secretary of the Treasury—performed a song and dance. It was based on the old vaudeville act of Gallagher and Shean and on the fact that the First Lady had just returned to the White House from a trip through the West, during which she had visited two of her sons and cast an absentee ballot.

It had been so funny and well received that the First Lady and Elinor Morgenthau had often been asked to repeat the performance. Finally, at a dinner for the benefit of the USO and particularly for the benefit of wounded naval officers, they did a similar song and dance again. It was a strictly private performance, but they felt they must revise the words to fit the situation five years later.

They met in the First Lady's study and became much amused over the new lines they were writing—

Mrs. Morgenthau:
Oh, Mrs. Roosevelt! Oh, Mrs. Roosevelt!
How much sugar does Mr. Churchill stir in his tea?

Mrs. Roosevelt:
Oh, Mrs. M., my dear, you've got it wrong I fear.
Mr. Churchill drinks like the Rambling Wrecks, and like them he drinks it clear!

Mrs. Morgenthau:
Oh, Mrs. R.! Oh, Mrs. R.! Please tell me Mr. Churchill's not a drunk!

Mrs. Roosevelt:
A drunk! Oh, never fear! He could drink till it's up to here! And never even lapse into a funk!

They sat laughing at these lines, by no means satisfied they would use them, when Bobby Kirkwal phoned.

Elinor Morgenthau left for home, promising to write more lines and telephone them later. Kirkwal walked through the

West Sitting Hall, where the President was presiding over his cocktail hour. He promised to come out and join in, after he'd reported some information to the First Lady.

She welcomed him into her study.

"We have an unhappy little Chinese girl, crying in her room on the third floor," he said.

"You didn't—"

"Only psychologically. But she told us a couple of interesting things."

"Such as?"

"T'sa Yuang-hung has a family in Peking—that is, a family in the hands of the Japanese."

"How, then, could he be a Kuomintang intelligence officer?" asked Mrs. Roosevelt. "Surely they wouldn't . . ."

"I can think of several explanations. One is that it isn't true, that he only told the girl that to win her sympathy so she would go to bed with him."

"The Generalissimo must know. T'sa Yuang-hung wouldn't tell that girl something he had managed to keep secret from Chiang Kai-shek."

"Assuming it's true," said Kirkwal.

"Perhaps we can find out. Maybe General Stilwell knows."

"We should ask. Now . . . Chin Yu-lin discovered during the course of the evening that T'sa Yuang-hung is well acquainted with Washington. He has been here before. He took her to Harvey's for dinner, and when J. Edgar Hoover came in, he pointed him out to her. He also told her a scandalous rumor about Hoover."

"I can imagine what that is."

"He could have been lying about that, too. But I can't think so. An American is likely to have seen a picture of Hoover, in a newspaper or in *Life;* and I don't think T'sa Yuang-hung would have dared to point at just any man and call him Hoover."

"What significance do you attach to this?" asked Mrs. Roosevelt.

"Well . . . no one chose to tell us that Madame Chiang's 'secretary' was a Kuomintang intelligence agent who had been in Washington before. Does that mean anything?"

"It's disingenuous at least," she said.

"I am beginning to wonder precisely what Weng Guo-fang is."

"Mr. Kirkwal," said the First Lady. "We

must focus our attention on the espionage element of this mystery. Even if some of Madame Chiang's staff are using their visit to enrich themselves by smuggling little red pills into our country . . . Well, that's very bad; but it's nothing compared to the harm that could be done in the Pacific."

"I'll focus on that, Ma'am," said Kirkwal.

Shortly after Kirkwal left, Mrs. Roosevelt dressed and departed for the National Guard Armory. A grand exhibition, billed as the Make-Do Show, was being held there, and she had been invited—together with many other celebrities—to tour the displays. The presence of celebrities was meant to attract press and newsreel attention; and, given the nature of the cause, the First Lady was happy to lend her presence.

The Make-Do Show was an exhibit of ways to cope with rationing and shortages, how to serve the nation in wartime by conserving all kinds of essential resources. On the way to the armory, Mrs. Roosevelt's limousine picked up Senator Truman and his wife and daughter, who would accompany her as she toured the exhibits.

"I'm looking forward to meeting some of the people I hear are going to be there," said the young Miss Truman. She was nineteen years old and the kind of young woman Mrs. Roosevelt instinctively liked: open and straightforward, like her father for whom the First Lady's respect had grown every year since he had come to Washington. "Ethel Merman. Al Jolson."

"Senator Taft's going to be there," said her father.

"I've met Senator Taft several times—plus enough other senators to last me a lifetime," said Miss Truman, with a throaty laugh under her voice.

As they walked through the doors and into the great open space of the Armory, flashbulbs popped and newsreel cameras whirred. "I can hear Lowell Thomas now," said Senator Truman; and quietly, to Mrs. Roosevelt and his wife and daughter only, he dropped his voice several registers and capably mimicked the tones of Lowell Thomas, who very likely would narrate the newsreel—

"As the great Make-Do Show opens in Washington, who should appear but— Of course. To be expected. No one but the peripatetic First Lady, Mrs. Eleanor Roosevelt! After all, what kind of show would it be without Mrs. Roosevelt?

"Entering the Armory with the First Lady is the United States Senator from Missouri, Henry Truman, accompanied by his wife and . . . And, oh yes! The attractive young woman is the senator's daughter, Miss Mary Beth Truman!

"They'll tour the exhibits and see how Americans can conserve the essential materials our country needs to win this war!"

The committee in charge of the exhibition hurried forward and led the First Lady and the Trumans into the show.

On a huge banner overhanging the whole exhibition was a slogan that had become ubiquitous since December 1941—

USE IT UP!
WEAR IT OUT!
MAKE IT DO,
OR DO WITHOUT!

The committee pointed the way to the automotive exhibit. The cameramen followed as Mrs. Roosevelt and the Truman family approached a 1938 Chevrolet truck, augmented on one side with an ungainly big steel box.

"What in the world is this contraption?" asked Senator Truman.

A man in a tattered gray suit, wearing white socks and black shoes, spoke to Mrs. Roosevelt instead of the senator. "Ma'am," he said. "This here's my charcoal-burning truck. I deliver coal with 'er, and I don't use no gasoline."

A smelly smoke was rising from a short stack on top of the box. The man opened a door on the bottom of the box, to show that a hot fire was burning inside. He climbed up on the truck and came down with two big chunks of charred wood, which he tossed into the fire before he closed the door. He climbed into the cab, put the truck in gear, and it moved off briskly. The man honked the horn to clear the way, and he made a circuit of the whole armory.

Some people cheered. Some stood aside resentfully as the truck, trailing smelly and probably poisonous fumes, made its way.

The man beamed as he climbed down from the cab. "Burning charcoal makes methane," he said. "Methane's what burns in gas stoves or furnaces. Pump that into the cylinders 'stead of gasoline vapors, and she runs fine. Takes a few adjustments."

"Why, that is perfectly marvelous," said Mrs. Roosevelt. "You make your deliveries and use none of the gasoline we need to fuel planes and tanks."

"Yes, Ma'am," said the man happily.

"We are grateful to you," she said.

The next exhibit was of a variety of devices meant to conserve tire rubber. Some of them were simply wooden wheels, fashioned to fit on cars or trucks. Others were wooden wheels to which various things had been nailed: the rubber remaining from totally worn-out tires, the soles of worn-out shoes and boots, even layers of glued paper.

Moving on, Mrs. Roosevelt and the Trumans met Ethel Merman in the food section, where women were demonstrating ways to cook appetizing meals without now-scarce butter and meat. She was sampling a cup of coffee when she recognized the First Lady.

"Mrs. Roose-vaalt!" she said in her distinctive voice, that could not come through except nasal and brassy, even if she wanted it otherwise—and burdened with a New York accent as well. "An honor!"

"I've seen you on the stage, Miss Merman," said Mrs. Roosevelt. "It is I who am honored. Let me present Senator Truman and Mrs. Truman and their daughter Margaret."

"Pleasure," said Ethel Merman. "Don't try the coffee. What they're trying to prove is that you can run water through your old grounds a second time, maybe a third time. Forget it!"

"Miss Truman is taking voice lessons," said Mrs. Roosevelt.

"Much good may it do you, kid. I sing on Broadway with a voice that'd make a voice coach puke."

"I'm thinking of opera," said Margaret Truman.

"Different," said Ethel Merman. "There, y' gotta be able to *sing*. Me, what I do is *belt!*"

Margaret Truman laughed. "I'd belt, if I could do it your way," she said.

Ethel Merman glanced at her watch. "Won't believe what I'm doin'," she said. "Five more minutes, I gotta get up on that stage over there and do it again."

"And what is that, Miss Merman?"

"Hoist my skirt up to here," she said, poking her legs with two fingers, about halfway between her knees and hips. "Let a gal paint my legs to make it look like I got nylons. Then take a bow and run to the ladies' room to wash it off so I can have it done again fifteen minutes later. An edifying spectacle, it ain't. What we do for our country . . ."

"I'd be glad to do it," said Margaret Truman.

"By damn, you'll join me, then. You're what?—fifteen, sixteen years younger'n me. You're the kind of gal ought to be doin' it anyway. C'mon, kiddo. I'll make a spectacle of you."

Agent Bobby Kirkwal had promised Mrs. Roosevelt he would direct all his attention to the espionage element of the

group of crimes—maybe related, maybe not related—they were trying to solve. He'd crossed his fingers, so to speak, when he gave the First Lady that promise. He was satisfied there was a relationship between the death of George Shen in the Map Room a week ago last Wednesday night and the sudden appearance of the little red pills in Washington. He couldn't yet even imagine what that relationship was, but he could not believe the two facts had happened in the same week because of coincidence.

In any case, Ed Kennelly had invited him to ride with him this Friday night.

"Tell ya, Bobby. Pills are all over. Seem to center on Seventh and G. China-town. This means—and whether I like it or not, whether it's got to do with anything you and I are interested in—that the District force has moved into Chinatown like the army movin' into North Africa. I handed pictures of George Shen to every man, sergeant up, workin' that beat. Might find—"

"That would be too much luck," said Kirkwal.

"Stuff doesn't work out by luck," said

Kennelly as he lit a Lucky. "Works out by leg work. I'm gonna do some tonight. Come or don't come."

"I'm supposed to report to Mrs. R. about midnight."

"Mebbe we'll have somethin' to report."

The Chinese community in Washington was not large. It was not like that in San Francisco or even that in New York, in that there were not enough young toughs to organize into gangs. It had in the city a reputation for cleanliness, industry, and honesty—the same as the other Chinatowns but this one unmarred by occasional outbursts of gang violence.

Miss Kung had remarked that Americans probably supposed all Chinese were laundrymen. Not so in Washington, where laundry was done almost exclusively by Negro women. The Chinese here sold exotic merchandise, operated restaurants, grew prosperous, lent money, invested, acquired property, and—to an extent that infuriated representatives of both the Kuomintang and the Communists—ignored

what was happening in a country to which they had no intention of returning. The District police were hardly aware of their existence, except for the distressing knowledge that some of the Chinese sold their exquisite young daughters: the ones they would someday send back to China.

The pills were something new.

"They damage everything," said Liu Yan.

The Venerable Liu Yan, as he was called in the Chinese community in Washington, was a patriarch in the ancient Chinese style. He wore the pigtail the post-Manchu governments had prohibited, together with a wispy white mustache and goatee. He wore silk: little, button-top hat, floor-length black gown embroidered with green-and-yellow dragons with bright red tongues and vines with leaves and flowers.

"These people are contemptible," the old man said. It was not clear who he was talking about: the criminals who imported the little red pills, or maybe even the Chiang regime. "They bring shame on us."

Kennelly and Kirkwal sat in an opulently furnished room scented with burning incense, behind a room Liu Yan referred to as his "counting room"—the room where he lent money, probably at usurious rates of interest, bought quantities of ginseng, sight unseen, on the assurance of the vendors that the roots were real, subscribed to partnerships in businesses and enterprises, and . . . No one knew all he did.

One of his granddaughters served tea. They drank from tiny cups with no handles. No sugar was offered. No cream. The tea was black as coffee, and strong.

Only now, when they had shared tea, did Liu Yan agree to examine the photographs Kennelly had asked him to scan.

He shook his head. "I do not know any of these men," he said after frowning for a moment over the photographs of Weng Guo-fang, T'sa Yuang-hung, and George Shen. "Nor of her," he added, handing over a picture of Chin Yu-lin.

The granddaughter had looked over his shoulder. "I have seen one of those men, Venerable Grandfather," she said. "Maybe two of them."

The old man glanced up at her, faintly reproving her intrusion. "Then speak, child," he said.

She reached down with a small, delicate hand and touched the photograph of T'sa Yuang-hung. "Our community is small," she said. "We notice strangers. I have seen this man on the street."

"Only this one?" Kirkwal asked.

"Yes."

"I must show you another picture," said Kennelly. "I am sorry. This one is a little gruesome."

He showed her a morgue photo of Liang P'ing—only of the face.

"Oh, yes!" she said, turning away. "He is dead there, yes? I have seen him, too. On the street."

"Where?"

"I saw him standing on the street in front of the Shanghai Import Company. I am sure of it. He stared at the window so intently that he made me wonder if he, Chinese as he obviously was, had never before seen Chinese things like those in the window. He had a . . . I don't know how to say it. He had a look of *evil* about him. Is it wrong to say this?"

Henry K'ang greeted the D.C. detective and the Secret Service agent with a reserved smile and a slight bow. He gestured with upturned palms at the variety of exotic merchandise offered in his store, the Shanghai Import Company. Even after they had introduced themselves, he seemed to hope they had come in to buy, maybe, an ivory stick, fashioned for use as a backscratcher, or perhaps a set of jade chessmen. When he saw they had come strictly on official business, he turned crisply businesslike.

He looked at the photographs of Weng Guo-fang, T'sa Yuang-hung, Liang P'ing, and Chin Yu-lin. "Yes," he said. "I have seen these men. Not the girl."

"Where did you see them?" Kennelly asked.

"Here," said K'ang. "They stopped in."

"Why?"

K'ang tapped the photograph of Weng Guo-fang. "This man," he said, "is a member of the party attending Madame Chiang Kai-shek, who, as you may know, is visiting at the White House this month. He bought a small quantity of incense, saying he was dissatisfied with the musty odors in his rooms."

"Incense . . ."

"This man—" K'ang pointed at the picture of T'sa Yuang-hung, "—purchased a silk jacket. He, too, is visiting from China and may also be on the staff of Madame Chiang. He said this kind of goods is not available now in China, and he professed himself as happy to be able to purchase the garment."

Kennelly put a finger on the picture of Liang P'ing: the morgue photo.

Henry K'ang raised his chin and frowned behind his big rimless, octagonal eyeglasses. "This man is not with the Chiang party. Nor is he from China. I would guess he is from New York. He came in here and asked me if I would be interested in selling some goods he had brought into the United States. When I asked what kind of goods he meant, he became crudely sly and said it was something on which I would make a great profit but he didn't want to name it unless I assured him I could keep a secret. I asked him if the goods were lawful. He asked if I cared. I said I did, definitely. He turned on his heel and walked out. A very bad kind. In any event," he added, raising his eyebrows, "it appears to have made no difference. The man in this picture is obviously dead."

"Why didn't you call the police?" asked Kennelly.

K'ang shrugged. "And report what?" he asked. "That a man had begun to talk about a possibly illegal transaction and had walked out of my store when I said I wasn't interested? And what would you have done if I had reported it, Captain? I would have given you a description, and you couldn't have found him. Or maybe you did. You haven't said how he comes to be dead."

"I have one more picture to show you," said Kennelly. He handed over a picture of George Shen: another morgue shot. "What about him?"

K'ang frowned hard. "This man is dead, too. What are you investigating, Captain?"

"Murder," said Kennelly.

"I have seen this man as well. He never came in here, but he was on the street and in restaurants in our neighborhood. As you know, Captain, ours is a small community. We know each other.

You have shown me pictures of four Chinese. None are of our community."

"Are you aware," Kennelly asked, "that a sudden flood of deadly drugs appears to be flowing out of your community?"

K'ang nodded. "I am well aware of it. Painfully aware, I might say. I hope you will stop it."

"I mean to," said Kennelly.

When they returned to the unmarked D.C. police car, a pair of young men stood beside it.

"Something we can do for you fellas?" Kennelly asked brusquely.

"Maybe," said one of them. "And maybe we can do something for you."

Kirkwal reflected that he had difficulty guessing the ages of Orientals. It seemed unlikely this pair were over draft age, yet here they were, not in the forces. They were slight but conspicuously brawny, wearing black overcoats and black hats. He guessed they were carrying pistols.

"Our names are not important, though we will give them to you if you want to know," said one of them. "It will be easier all around if you just call me Pete. Have you ever heard of an organization called Hop Sing?"

"I believe that's what's called a tong," said Kennelly. "No?"

The man smiled. "It is called that. It is also *called* Hop Sing. There is no such organization as Hop Sing, Captain Kennelly. It is a myth. On the other hand, a few of the men of this community do have a social club, which has no name at all, and are interested in a number of things for the good of our community. We would like to offer you our services."

"What can you do for us?" Kennelly asked.

"We suppose you are here because of the little red pills."

"Not a bad guess," said Kennelly.

"We are prepared to do whatever is necessary to stop this plague."

"Does that include killing the guy who brought the pills into the neighborhood?"

Pete nodded. "We could have killed him, gladly and without hesitation, if we had caught him before he dumped his deadly merchandise. We only regret we didn't."

"You better leave that kind of stuff to the police. If you'd killed him, I'd have had to haul you in for murder."

Pete smiled. "I think not," he said. "You wouldn't have found the body. You wouldn't have known what happened."

"Supposin' that's so, what are we talkin' about now?" asked Kennelly.

"We can identify some of those who are selling the pills," said Pete. "We know our streets."

"What I want is the wholesaler," said Kennelly.

"And to find him, you pick up the retailers. I imagine you have means to persuade them to tell you where they bought their supply."

Kirkwal had to return to the White House. Kennelly, reinforced by Detective Sergeant Hupp and a car with two uniformed officers, went with Pete and his friend in search of dealers in little red pills.

It was midnight when Mrs. Roosevelt met with Kirkwal in her study. She ordered coffee and sandwiches and a bottle of Scotch from the kitchen.

He gave her the new information: that the men in Madame Chiang's company had been seen in Washington's small Chinatown, that Kennelly was out tracking down the pill sellers.

"I have a strong feeling we're going to trace the pills to Liang P'ing at least and maybe to T'sa Yuang-hung—maybe even old Weng Guo-fang. God grant us that the Madame herself is not involved."

"God grant us that this line of inquiry leads us closer to a solution to the George Shen murder," said Mrs. Roosevelt.

XIII

Mrs. Morgenthau:
Oh, Mrs. Roosevelt! Oh, Mrs. Roosevelt!
We hear that John L. Lewis drives you mad!

Mrs. Roosevelt:
Drives me mad? Oh, not at all!
It's just that he has so much gall.
But under those brows he's really not so bad.

Mrs. Morgenthau:
Now, is that really true?

Mrs. Roosevelt:
Oh yes, it's really quite true.

Mrs. Morgenthau:
Positively, Mrs. Roosevelt?

Mrs. Roosevelt:
Absolutely, Mrs. M!

The President, at her invitation, had stopped by the First Lady's study before going down to the West Wing, and the two women had sung their verses for him. He sat in his wheelchair, laughing heartily, cigarette atilt in his trademark holder.

"Babs," he said, "I think you missed your calling. You make a better vaudevillian than you do detective."

"That's unkind, Frank," said Elinor Morgenthau. "Eleanor has solved some pretty tough mysteries."

He gave a placatory nod. "Hawkshaw the Detective, right here under my own roof. Any word, incidentally, on the problem from a week ago last Wednesday. I really don't want to have to move a task force."

"A little progress maybe," said Mrs. Roosevelt. "Nothing important enough to tell you."

The President shook his head. "I'm afraid I'm going to have to call in big guns, Babs," he said. "Turn the whole thing over to Naval Intelligence maybe."

"I understand," she said.

"I don't," said Elinor Morgenthau. "I've no idea what you're talking about, and I guess you'd tell me if you wanted me to know."

"Sorry, Elinor," said the President. "You'll be happier if you don't."

He wheeled himself out of the First Lady's study toward the elevator. Bells began to ring downstairs. The President was coming!

For the two women he left behind, it was difficult to return their attention to writing comic verses.

"It's something serious, isn't it?" Elinor Morgenthau asked quietly.

Mrs. Roosevelt sighed. "Yes, rather."

A few minutes later, Agent Bobby Kirkwal arrived, accompanied by Major John Bentz, the commander of the army guard unit for the White House. Elinor Morgenthau went out in the West Sitting Hall to continue working on the verses while Mrs. Roosevelt had a serious conversation.

"Is it as I thought?" asked the First Lady.

"Yes, Ma'am," said Major Bentz. "Since December 1941, a log has been kept of everyone who enters or leaves the White House grounds, day or night. Most of the time, only the northwest gate is open."

"And you have brought me the log for Wednesday, February seventeenth?"

"Yes, Ma'am. As you asked."

"I appreciate it," she said. "I don't want to mention what it is, since I might look rather silly if I prove wrong. But I want to look through this log. Major, please have available the man—or men—who were on duty that day."

"Yes, Ma'am."

"Mr. Kirkwal . . . Did Captain Kennelly have any success last night?"

"He surely did. He *surely* did."

And still was. Riding through the streets with the man who called himself Pete, Kennelly had picked up two men who were selling the little red pills. One was Chinese. One was not. His interrogation technique was not different from what he had used on Fuzzy Cairns. Only they had broken faster. The Chinese knew the name of the man who had sold him the pills.

Henry K'ang.

Kennelly was not surprised.

A squad of officers raided the Shanghai Import Company before dawn. They found no red pills. They arrested Henry K'ang, and for five hours he had sat in the basement interrogation room as Cairns had done—until he confessed.

"I am not certain," said Mrs. Roosevelt, "I can place much credence in confessions obtained this way. I am afraid a man in his circumstances would confess to anything, out of fear."

At Kennelly's invitation, she had come to the jail in mid-morning, to see Henry K'ang and hear him talk.

She saw him, and could hear him. He could not see her, or hear her. She and Kirkwal sat in a darkened room behind a two-way mirror. Kennelly confronted K'ang under bright lights. Though he didn't know it, a microphone picked up what he said. His every word was being recorded on eighteen-inch phonograph disks, the same as were used to transcribe radio programs, and his voice came to the First Lady and Kirkwal through headphones.

Henry K'ang wore blue-denim dungarees, far too large for him. A wide leather belt circled his waist. The links of his handcuffs were passed through a brass ring securely sewn to the belt, so he could not lift his hands away from his waist. The wide legs of his dungarees were tightly cinched to his ankles by his leg irons. He hung his head to shield his eyes from the bright lights shining on him.

"I cannot approve of this," said Mrs. Roosevelt. "The man looks exhausted."

"Ed Kennelly's response would be that the pills he's sold have killed at least one person already, and probably more," said Kirkwal.

"But . . . can we *believe* what a man in that circumstance says?"

"Let's find out."

Kennelly sat facing K'ang, comfortably, in a wooden armchair. He had taken off his coat and sat in his shirtsleeves, revealing the revolver in his leather shoulder holster. In the overbright light of the interrogation room, his complexion looked ruddier than ever, and his white hair contrasted against it even more than usual. He snapped his Zippo and lit a Lucky.

"Okay, Henry," he said almost gently. "You've told me the story, but this is for the record. This is where you make a record of being a cooperative or uncooperative prisoner."

K'ang did not raise his face.

"Now, Henry, you're gonna have to look at me. I don't like to talk to a man who doesn't look at me."

K'ang lifted his chin and stared apprehensively at Kennelly.

"Little red pills," said the big Irish detective. "What are they, Henry? What's in 'em?"

"I don't know for sure," said K'ang in a thin voice. "They're made out of opium. They have opium in them."

"What happens to people who swallow them?"

"They get that feeling you get from using opium," said K'ang.

"They get addicted?"

"Maybe. I never saw any before this batch. I don't know what they do, for sure."

"Who sold pills to Fuzzy Cairns?"

"Not me. It had to be one of my men."

"How many men do you have out sellin' pills?"

"Three."

"How many pills do you have, all told?"

"I bought a thousand."

"What'd you pay for 'em?"

"Two dollars each. I put them with my sellers for four dollars each, and they sold them for eight or ten dollars apiece, whatever they could get."

"A plague of poison," said Kennelly.

"No. Not really. You have to remember, Captain, that use of opium is cultural with us. Chinese people have used it for centuries. Some overuse it and die. Most use it very much like Americans use alcohol, for a small pleasure, relief from the cares of the day. You say a woman died from using the pills. She must have used far too many. One pill produces nothing more serious than euphoria—followed sometimes by a headache."

Kennelly rose from his chair and walked behind the chained man. K'ang twisted his head around and tried to keep a nervous eye on him.

"The pregnant question, Henry. Where did you get the little red pills?"

"I was visited about a week ago by a man who told me he had a quantity of them and wanted to sell them to me. We talked for some time about it. I knew what the pills were. I'd heard of the little red pills. I decided it was an easy way to make a bit of profit. That was a mistake. But I did it."

"You've identified the man who sold them to you, from his picture."

"Yes, the man you named Liang P'ing."

"You still insist you've never seen George Shen?"

"I swear I never saw that man."

"Or T'sa Yuang-hung?"

"Never."

"Or Weng Guo-fang?"

"Never."

Kennelly glanced at the two-way mirror, at Mrs. Roosevelt and Kirkwal in fact.

"You keep changing your story. Anyway—makes no difference. I'm afraid I have some bad news for you, Henry."

K'ang twisted around and stared up anxiously at Kennelly.

"Yeah. We found the rest of your pills.

A thousand? You're a stinkin' little liar, Henry. You had more than eight thousand of them left. Now how many of them did you really buy?"

"No! Somebody has stashed 'em on me! Where'd you find—?"

"A green '39 Plymouth. You wanna deny it's your car?"

K'ang shook his head.

Kennelly grinned. "In the innertube of the spare tire. You'd been in a hell of a pickle, Henry, if you'd had a flat. Now what was it you paid for your supply of pills?"

K'ang closed his eyes. "Twenty thousand dollars," he said glumly.

"How'd you pay? Check? Cash?"

"Cash. Hundred-dollar bills."

"You gave Liang P'ing twenty thousand in hundreds?"

K'ang nodded. He tugged on his handcuffs. "What you gonna do to me?"

"You wanta know if you're gonna get out of Leavenworth before you die? That depends on whether you tell me the truth or not."

"What else *can* I tell you, Captain?"

"Who *was* Liang P'ing, anyway?"

"He worked for Madame Chiang. He

was once a Shanghai waterfront gangster. When he left China, he bought as many of the opium pills as he could carry, to sell in the States."

"How many deliveries did he make to you, Henry?"

"Just one. He brought them all at once."

"When?"

"Monday."

"How was he carrying them? In a suitcase?"

"No. In the lining of his overcoat."

"We found nine thousand plus in your car. You had ten thousand originally, at least. They'd weigh almost fifty pounds. I don't think a man could walk through the White House gate carrying ten thousand pills, weighing fifty pounds, in the lining of his overcoat and not be noticed."

"Actually . . . actually he came twice."

Kennelly grabbed K'ang by the fabric at the throat of his dungarees and lifted him off the chair. Then he slammed him back down. "You're diggin' your grave deeper and deeper," he growled. "To leave the White House a person has to sign out, then sign back in. Liang P'ing left the

White House Monday evening, all right. But he never came back."

K'ang's lips shuddered, and tears glistened in his eyes. "There was another man," he said hoarsely.

"Which one?"

"T'sa Yuang-hung. He was a partner with Liang. The two of them invested in the pills and—"

"How about the old man?"

"No. Not the old man. Just the two of them."

"So, how much cash was Liang P'ing carrying when he left you?"

"Ten thousand. He delivered half the pills. T'sa Yuang-hung had already delivered half. I paid him ten thousand."

"I still don't believe you," said Kennelly. He glanced at his watch. "We'll lock you up for a while and talk to you later. Get used to a cell. That's how you'll be livin' for the next twenty years."

Kennelly came around and sat with Mrs. Roosevelt and Kirkwal on the other side of the mirror, in a small, grim room lighted only—though brightly enough—by the light coming through the mirror from the interrogation room.

"Figures," said Kennelly. "T'sa Yuang-hung went out Monday afternoon. Liang P'ing went out Monday evening. Both of them made deliveries to K'ang. When Liang left the Shanghai Trading Company, he was carrying a lot of money. A *lot* of money. He splashed some of it around and got robbed and killed."

"Then where is the money brought back by T'sa Yuang-hung?" asked Mrs. Roosevelt. "You didn't find it when you searched his room."

"I think we're gonna have to search all their stuff," said Kennelly.

"I am wondering," said the First Lady, "if I am not obliged to tell Madame Chiang what is going on."

"I would rather not think she already knows what is going on," said Kirkwal.

"We benefit from a fortunate coincidence, anyway. The Chiang party is leaving tomorrow, so the President and I are entertaining them at lunch today. We have invited them all: Madame Chiang, the Kungs, Weng Guo-fang, and T'sa Yuang-hung. The two maids are having lunch as well, with some of the kitchen staff they have so much annoyed during their visit."

"With the whole crowd at lunch, we can go through everything they've got," said Kennelly.

"With great care and subtlety, Captain Kennelly," said Mrs. Roosevelt. "With great care and subtlety."

"I'll bring in four or five agents to work on it," said Kirkwal.

"I may tell you," said Mrs. Roosevelt, "that I have begun to develop a definite theory about this case. I will reserve it a bit yet, until I feel more certain. But the solution may not be far off."

On the eve of her departure from the White House, for a nationwide tour, Madame Chiang Kai-shek would dine with some of her most fervid supporters, the men the President called the China lobby. The host for the dinner was Henry Luce. The President and Mrs. Roosevelt would not attend. In fact, they hadn't been invited. Madame Chiang's final meal in the White House was the Saturday luncheon. Though it was lunch and not dinner, the meal was served in the State Dining Room, to guests that included Generals Marshall and Arnold, Admirals King and Leahy, Secretary of State Hull, Vice President Wallace, Harry Hopkins, Bernard Baruch—also the wives of many of these men.

Just before she went down to the dining room, Mrs. Roosevelt received a call from Grace Tully, one of the President's secretaries, saying the President wanted her to stop by the Oval Office for a moment before the luncheon.

She walked into the Oval Office as the President was signing the last of a pile of documents.

"Take a look at this," he said, handing her a decoded telegram.

MOST SECRET FOR THE PRESIDENT ONLY.

I regret that I was not aware when I responded to your earlier inquiry that the subject you inquired about does indeed have a family in a city in enemy hands. The Generalissimo is aware of it, so I assume Madame must be aware of it too.

Remainder follows in another code.

MOST SECRET FOR THE PRESIDENT ONLY.

must be aware of it too. (This ends message in another code.) Subject may be under extreme personal pressure to betray. Has worked effectively, so far as I can learn, but could be traitor. Intelligence department here so inept that an elephant could walk through headquarters unnoticed.

Stilwell, Lieutenant General

The President put aside his pen and shoved the signed documents to the front of his desk. "Does that answer an important question?" he asked.

Mrs. Roosevelt nodded. "Early this morning, I said we'd made no great progress. I'm beginning to think the solution is in sight."

"Shall I move the task force?"

She smiled. "You're not ready to move any task force yet. But if you were, I'd say no, don't move it, not yet."

The President enjoyed official meals with diplomatic impact. Tuna-salad sandwiches could hardly be served, nor could sickly-sweet New York State wines. Champagne had to be served—*French* champagne. And for this luncheon, roast beef with Bordeaux.

He toasted Chinese-American friendship.

Madame Chiang rose and toasted it, too.

Upstairs, a squad of Secret Service agents and two D.C. detectives were going through the baggage of the Chinese diplomatic party. Uniformed White House guards had closed the stairs and elevators. No one could reach the second or third floors.

Kirkwal himself, with Kennelly, took charge of the search in Madame Chiang's personal suite.

Downstairs:

"It has been *such* a pleasure to have you as our guests in the White House."

"You really must visit China. Our country is not at its best right now, but the Generalissimo and I will cherish the opportunity to show you as much hospitality as you have shown us."

Upstairs:

"Interesting. Getting right down to it, the wife of a gismo wears the same kind of underwear as the wife of an American bus driver."

"Not quite."

"Smells good, I must say."

Downstairs:

"The friendship and trust we have further cemented these two weeks will endure through war and peace."

Upstairs:

"What do we do about this? The damned maids have lifted a dozen silver spoons, plus a goddamn silver sugar and creamer."

"Leave it. It's worth more than some spoons and a tea service to keep this search secret."

Downstairs:

"Our two countries, our two cultures, will continue to move closer and closer together."

Upstairs:

"What the hell is this? Look. Little ivory egg. Damn! It's hollow, and something's rolling around inside!"

"Mercury. It's mercury rolling around inside."

"What the hell for?"

"Ed, if you don't know what it's for, never mind. I'll explain later. Let's get up to the third floor and see what the boys are finding in the luggage."

"What we *didn't* find is what's important," said Kennelly when he and Kirkwal joined Mrs. Roosevelt after the luncheon, in her study. "No money. No more pills. If T'sa Yuang-hung came back to the White House Monday afternoon with ten thousand bucks in cash, where's that money?"

"I'm beginning to believe," said Mrs. Roosevelt, "that no money was paid for the pills."

"How do you figure that?" asked Kennelly. "Why would they hand over the pills without—"

"I've an idea," she said. "The fact that you found no money makes sense to me."

"Would you mind telling us what your idea is?" asked Kirkwal.

"I'd rather you continued thinking independently," she said. "You may develop a different and better idea."

"We did find one thing we expected,"

said Kennelly. "T'sa Yuang-hung's overcoat has hidden pockets sewed in the lining."

"Yes," said Mrs. Roosevelt. "That was to be expected. And so, undoubtedly, did Liang P'ing's."

"Something else that oughta be no surprise," said Kennelly. "We didn't find any silk jacket, either."

"I'm afraid the significance of that eludes me," said Mrs. Roosevelt.

"When we first went in to see Henry K'ang," Kirkwal explained, "he admitted T'sa Yuang-hung had been in his store, but he said he came in to buy a silk jacket."

Mrs. Roosevelt frowned. "Why do you suppose he admitted T'sa Yuang-hung had been in his place of business?"

"He admitted that Weng Guo-fang and Liang P'ing had been there, too," said Kirkwal.

"Henry K'ang's a smart customer," said Kennelly. "He figured we *knew* one or more of the guys we asked him about had been in the store. Routine police procedure. Ask a question you already know the answer to. Trip the guy up in a lie. K'ang may not have looked too smart through that mirror this morning, but he's too smart to get caught in *that* little old trap. Anyway, he *was* too smart, before we sweated him."

The telephone rang. Mrs. Roosevelt picked it up. "Fine," she said. "Send them up."

"Should we leave?" asked Kirkwal.

"No, not at all," she said. "That was Major Bentz. He is sending up a soldier and a White House police officer: the ones who were on duty at the northwest gate a week ago last Wednesday afternoon and evening. In a few minutes we are, I believe, going to have the solution to our mystery."

XIV

"I apologize for the hour," said Mrs. Roosevelt. "The reason for it will become apparent."

The hour was midnight. Assembled in the Cabinet Room, seated around the cabinet table, were—

The President at the south end of the table, and Mrs. Roosevelt at the north end.

To the President's right on the east side of the table, Madame Chiang Kai-shek. To her right and on down the east side of the table, Weng Guo-fang, T'sa Yuang-hung, and Chin Yu-lin.

To Mrs. Roosevelt's right on the west side of the table, Agent Robert Kirkwal, then Captain David Bloom of Naval Intelligence, Henry K'ang in prison dungarees and handcuffs, and Captain Edward Kennelly.

A stenographer with a Stenotype machine sat at a small table behind Chin Yu-lin, recording all that was said.

The President spoke to Madame Chiang. "We regret the inconvenience to you," he said. "We would have met earlier, except that we could not meet until you returned from your dinner."

Madame Chiang nodded crisply and said, "Mrs. Roosevelt warned me late this afternoon that she would appreciate my attendance at a midnight meeting. I am confident she would not have called it except for some very good reason."

The First Lady of China was dressed in her usual style: high-necked silk dress with slit skirt—except that this one was white with patterns of tiny pearls sewn on it. She wore an exquisite jade necklace and a huge ring of jade and diamonds. She had, in fact, not changed since she returned from Henry Luce's dinner.

She made an interesting contrast with the President, whose gray suit had wrinkled over the course of a long day.

"I don't usually attend these sessions my wife calls. This one, though, has war significance. It also has diplomatic significance. I hope I can count on all of you to keep everything we say tonight totally confidential."

Madame Chiang raised her chin and stared hard at Henry K'ang. "Including him?" she asked coldly.

Kennelly grinned. "Henry won't say a word. His only chance of getting out of Leavenworth before he's carried out depends on his telling the truth and keeping secrets."

"Well, then," said Madame Chiang. "Why are we here?"

Mrs. Roosevelt spoke. "I imagine you know, Madame—though we didn't tell you—that on the first evening of your visit, a murder was committed in the White House. Not only that, it was committed in the Map Room, not very far from the doors to your suite. We were appalled. We were deeply concerned for your safety. We didn't tell you because we didn't want to put on your shoulders an additional burden of worry."

"Or embarrass yourselves," said Madame Chiang dryly.

"Or embarrass ourselves," Mrs. Roosevelt agreed.

"It might be well, I think," said the

President, "to reserve discussion of embarrassment for later."

Madame Chiang's flashing glance showed that she had some idea what he meant.

"The man who was murdered in the Map Room," Mrs. Roosevelt went on, all but ignoring the exchange between the President and Madame Chiang, "was named George Shen. He was a Chinese from San Francisco, but he had spent some time in Japan and spoke fluent Japanese. Our investigators found on his body what proved to be a message in a Japanese code. It was decoded. The message suggested the possibility of a Japanese naval movement into the Indian Ocean."

"How very convenient," said Madame Chiang. "A Japanese spy gets himself murdered in the White House while carrying a message in a code you have broken."

"Altogether *too* convenient," said Mrs. Roosevelt. "And yet, too suggestive to be ignored. The questions were: who was this man, and how did he get into the White House?"

"And who killed him, I should suppose."

"Yes. Though we thought the answers to the first two questions would probably answer the third."

"So who killed him?" asked Madame Chiang.

"Step by step," said Mrs. Roosevelt. "The unraveled mystery is more convincing than a mere statement."

"I have observed," said Weng Guofang quietly, "that the entrances to the White House are carefully guarded."

Mrs. Roosevelt nodded at the elderly man. He was wearing his gray suit tonight and somehow looked as if he might withdraw within it like a turtle into its shell, and disappear. He closed his eyes. It was not plain if he was concentrating or nodding off.

"As Mr. Weng has observed," Mrs. Roosevelt continued, "the first difficult question was: how did George Shen enter the White House? That baffled us for a while. And we were distracted by other questions. But this morning I found out. Do you want to explain it, Mr. Weng? Or shall I?"

Weng Guo-fang opened his eyes, not with alarm, just with subdued curiosity.

"Are you suggesting," asked Madame Chiang, "that the Little Father here—?"

"Do you want to explain it, Mr. Weng?" Mrs. Roosevelt persisted.

"I shall be curious to hear what you have to say, dear lady."

"Since December 1941," she said, "no one enters or leaves the White House simply at will. No one may enter without permission. When a person enters, he or she signs a log at the gate. Even I sign the log. I believe the President doesn't, and I believe he is the only one who does not."

"Even I have signed the log," said Madame Chiang.

"Winston Churchill is the only one who does not," said the President, smiling as he lit a cigarette.

"You left the White House, Mr. Weng, at 4:37 P.M. on Wednesday of last week. You returned at 5:48. You signed out, and you signed in. When you returned, you were accompanied by another man. Who was that?"

"Liang P'ing," said Weng Guo-fang.

"And when did he go out?" asked

Mrs. Roosevelt. "He did not leave the White House with you, did he? He returned with you, but he did not leave with you."

Weng Guo-fang nodded. "I encountered him as I walked across Lafayette Park."

"Ah . . ." said Mrs. Roosevelt. "When you reached the gate, the guards didn't know him. They knew you, because you had gone in and out many times—having arrived at the White House in advance of Madame Chiang to supervise arrangements for her visit. So the army corporal and the uniformed White House policeman at the gate knew you. They asked who Mr. Liang P'ing was, and you told them. Is that not correct?"

Weng Guo-fang nodded.

"But the man with you was not Mr. Liang P'ing," said Mrs. Roosevelt.

"Of course he was!"

"No. He was not Mr. Liang. How do I know that? Because Mr. Liang P'ing had not signed out. Mr. T'sa Yuang-hung had signed out earlier and earlier returned. But Mr. Liang had not signed out. In fact, from the time he arrived with Madame Chiang's party on Wednesday, he never left the White House until Monday evening, when he signed out, never to return. You brought someone else into the White House, identifying him as Mr. Liang. Who was it, Mr. Weng?"

"It seems to me you place a great deal of confidence in your gate guards," said Madame Chiang. "You are making a serious accusation against my friend, on the basis of the statement of a couple of . . . of . . ."

The President supplied the word she may have been looking for. "Peasants, Madame?" he asked.

"Workmen," she said.

"The corporal and the policeman have looked at the morgue photographs," said Mrs. Roosevelt. "In fact, they had looked at them before. They are not sure who they saw. But they are sure of one thing. *No Liang P'ing signed out.*"

"I am highly skeptical," said Madame Chiang,

"What is more," said Mrs. Roosevelt, "the Wednesday evening 'Liang P'ing' signed his name very differently from the Monday evening Liang P'ing."

"This means," interjected Bobby Kirk-wal, "that there was an extra person in the White House last Wednesday evening. And that extra person never signed out, with any name. He didn't have to. He was carried out."

"Don't people carry identification documents?" asked Madame Chiang.

"Do you?" asked Kirkwal. "Have you been asked to prove who you are? Others are, generally, if they are not recognized by the gate guards. But we had extended diplomatic courtesy to you and your party."

"Even supposing," said Weng Guo-fang, "that I did help someone else to enter the premises, of what significance is that fact? I could have had a variety of reasons for bringing someone in."

"The significance, Mr. Fang," said Ed Kennelly, "is that you lied to get this man in."

"I have never been called a liar!" Weng protested.

"Have people always overlooked it?" asked Kennelly. "But there's somethin' more important. After you brought that guy in, there were two P'ings in the White

House, the real P'ing who'd never gone out, plus the guy you brought in callin' P'ing. The real P'ing was here all along. The other guy went out under a sheet. You're somethin' more than just a liar, Mr. Fang."

"Mr. *Weng!*" cried Madame Chiang. "His name is Weng Guo-fang!"

"We can use either name on the indictment," said Kennelly.

"Indictment for what, Captain?" Madame Chiang demanded coldly.

"Murder," said Kennelly.

The President sat and calmly watched as Madame Chiang rose and announced that she was leaving this meeting, taking with her the members of her staff who joined her in being deeply offended at the accusation leveled at her senior adviser by a lowly Irish police captain.

"Please . . ." said Mrs. Roosevelt. "You should hear what we have to tell you. It may be more important to you than it is to us."

"And why would that be?" Madame Chiang demanded loftily.

"Because the Irish cop," grunted Kennelly, "also accuses your 'senior adviser' of being a Jap spy."

Madame Chiang sat down. "I dearly, dearly hope you can justify yourself, Captain Kennelly," she hissed. "I have many powerful friends in this country."

"You may have fewer, Madame Chiang," said the President, "when the word is circulated that you brought, not just one but three, Japanese spies into the White House. Four, actually; two are dead."

"I shall listen," she conceded.

"Better speak up, Weng old boy," said the President.

"By whom am I accused?" asked Weng Guo-fang. "On what evidence?"

"Mr. K'ang," said Mrs. Roosevelt to the terrified prisoner who had been glancing back and forth in utter horror from Kennelly to Madame Chiang to the President to Mrs. Roosevelt and back to Kennelly. "Your crime is treason. The penalty is death. Very likely, murder can be added."

K'ang sobbed and choked. He raised his manacled hands and rubbed his eyes.

"This man has been . . . beaten," said Weng Guo-fang. "Intimidated."

"Mr. T'sa," said Mrs. Roosevelt to T'sa Yuang-hung. "How much did Mr. K'ang pay you for the pills you delivered to him?"

"Pills?"

"Pills, fella," said Kennelly. "Little red pills."

"Little red pills!" cried Madame Chiang. "What are you saying? The Japanese—"

"Until this week," said Kennelly, "we hadn't seen the Jap little red pills in Washington. Then suddenly K'ang has got ten thousand of them. And your friend Mr. Hung has got big extra pockets sewed inside his overcoat. Like what guys used to carry bottles in, in the old days. He went to see Henry K'ang Monday afternoon. His sign-out and sign-in is on the gate log. Then P'ing leaves the White House and goes to see Henry K'ang—only he never comes back. Then a woman dies from taking those pills. That gets the District police very upset."

"What is more," said Kirkwal, "the body of Liang P'ing is found in the Anacostia River the next morning."

Madame Chiang swung around in her

chair; and, looking past Weng Guo-fang, she glared icily at T'sa Yuang-hung and asked, "What have you done, Yuang? Is this how you repay?"

"They have no evidence of anything they're suggesting," said T'sa Yuang-hung. "None, unless you wish to take the word of that . . . that browbeaten souvenir merchant."

"What would T'sa Yuang-hung be repaying?" the President asked Madame Chiang.

"Our confidence in him," she said. "His family was in Peking and failed to escape when the Japanese overran the city. He came to us at Chungking, pleading for help. We granted our trust."

"Did you trust Liang P'ing also?" the President asked.

Madame Chiang glared at Weng Guo-fang. "He was with us because you wanted him."

"A useful man," said Weng calmly.

"What did he do that cost him his life?" asked Madame Chiang.

Weng Guo-fang and T'sa Yuang-hung said nothing. They shrugged without shrugging.

"Let me guess," said Mrs. Roosevelt. "He demanded money. Is that not so, Mr. K'ang?"

"K'ang scowled at T'sa Yuang-hung. "I'm not going to carry all this by myself," he said.

"Whatever it is you're carrying, you'd like to find someone else to carry part of it for you," said Weng Guo-fang. "You'll accuse anyone."

Madame Chiang sneered toward K'ang. "He doesn't make a very persuasive witness," she said.

"Fortunately, we don't have to rely on him," said Mrs. Roosevelt. "It has been established, on incontrovertible evidence, that Mr. Weng brought an unauthorized someone into the White House. So far he has managed to evade telling us who, and why."

Madame Chiang spun on Weng Guo-fang. "I command you to answer those questions!"

The old man smiled gently. "Your commands mean no more here than they do in China—that is, anywhere in China but Chungking, and not even in all of that." He spoke to the President. "Nor do her husband's. She talks to you about the Generalissimo's three hundred divisions. The poor man couldn't raise three. And if he had them, he'd use them for showy parades, nothing more."

Madame Chiang shrieked, *"Then to whom does your loyalty extend, old eunuch?"*

"Not to the heirs of those who emasculated a twelve-year-old boy," said Weng Guo-fang.

"My husband is not an heir to the Manchus!"

"He is not, perhaps. You are. You are an heir of everything that is arbitrary and cruel and corrupt."

"I believe, Mr. Weng," said Mrs. Roosevelt, "that you have just confessed to being a Japanese agent."

"I have confessed to nothing," said Weng Guo-fang.

"He has condemned himself to death!" yelled Madame Chiang.

"Who will carry out the sentence?" asked Weng Guo-fang, turning against her a placid, heavy-lidded face.

Ed Kennelly rose and walked around the table, behind the President and along

the east side of the table until he was behind T'sa Yuang-hung. "I'll take your pistol,
Hung," he said.

"Will you really?" asked T'sa Yuang-
hung.

"He will, really," said Bobby Kirkwal,
leveling a small automatic at T'sa from the
other side of the table.

Kennelly reached inside T'sa's jacket
and lifted out a snub-nose revolver. "Mr.
Fang?" he asked. "You have one?"

Weng Guo-fang shook his head, but
Kennelly patted him down.

Mrs. Roosevelt shook her head and
spoke to the President. "Matters don't
usually get this dramatic," she said.

"Diplomatic privilege, Mr. President,"
said Kirkwal. "Otherwise we wouldn't allow
a man in your presence with a weapon."

"Regard diplomatic privilege as canceled in that respect," said the President.

"Madame Chiang," said Mrs. Roosevelt. "I have to make an embarrassing
confession. While we were at lunch today,
a search was made of your party's luggage
stored on the third floor, also of the rooms
occupied by Mr. T'sa, Mr. Weng, and Mr.
Liang."

"Don't apologize. I would be disappointed in you if you hadn't."

"What we didn't find was more significant than what we did. Specifically, we found no great amount of money, even though Mr. K'ang says he paid Mr. T'sa and Mr. Liang twenty thousand dollars for little red pills."

Madame Chiang stared for a moment at Henry K'ang. "Considering the treason spoken by my senior adviser, why should I be any less persuaded by the testimony of K'ang than the testimony of Weng? But what is the significance of *not* finding twenty thousand dollars?"

Kirkwal spoke. "We've done a little looking into K'ang's accounts. He might have had that much money under his mattress, but it's unlikely. He has a checking and savings account in a bank. They have never had as much as twenty thousand dollars in them. We much doubt that Henry K'ang could have paid twenty thousand dollars for pills."

"And the significance of that, please?" Madame Chiang persisted.

"Mr. K'ang paid nothing for the pills," said Mrs. Roosevelt. "They were brought here by three Japanese agents—Mr. Weng Guo-fang, Mr. T'sa Yuang-hung, and Mr. Liang P'ing—and handed over to the chief local Japanese agent, Mr. Henry K'ang, for nothing. And why? They were to be sold in Washington, and the money obtained for them was to fund Japanese espionage activities in this city."

"That is a guess, is it not?" asked Madame Chiang.

"It's been done that way in other places," said Captain Bloom. "The Japanese are producing the pills in immense quantities. They want to make addicts, to demoralize armies chiefly, but civilian populations as well."

"That is what the Opium Wars were all about," said Madame Chiang.

"Yes," Bloom agreed. "So they distribute millions of pills free. Others, they sell. They financed their fifth column in Singapore that way. And one in Jakarta. Those we know about. There are undoubtedly others."

"It works damned well," said Kennelly. "The money their spies use is in small denominations, wrinkled old bills—what's paid over by thousands of addicts. They can smuggle the pills in easier than they can money, and they get money that can't be traced."

Mrs. Roosevelt turned to Henry K'ang. "Is this correct, Mr. K'ang?" she asked.

K'ang nodded. "It was the first time I was asked to do anything like this. Until now, I sent to my contact only information like where the antiaircraft guns were on the White House grounds, what lights had been extinguished because of the war, how much butter or meat an American family can buy each month . . ."

"Then came the big boys, hey, Henry?" said Kennelly.

K'ang sighed and nodded. "You have surmised correctly," he said to Mrs. Roosevelt.

"You're in about as big trouble as a man can get, Henry," said Kennelly. "I see two death sentences. Your only chance—"

"Yes . . . I know. I killed Liang. I arranged it, anyway. He ordered it—" Nodding toward T'sa Yuang-hung. "Can you guess why?"

"He wanted money for the pills he delivered to you," said Mrs. Roosevelt.

"Yes. So he was sentenced to death,

by those two: Weng Guo-fang and T'sa Yuang-hung."

"Traitors!" shrieked Madame Chiang.

"It is true," K'ang mumbled, "that I could not have raised twenty thousand dollars. Or even ten. But Liang professed to believe that all Americans were rich and said he would not turn over his pills unless I made him a substantial payment. T'sa Yuang-hung had warned me Liang might do this and had ordered me to be prepared to kill him if he did."

"You gave him a little party, to get him good and drunk and easier to kill," said Kennelly.

"I wasn't prepared to kill a man," said K'ang. "I had to leave my place of business and contact the men who would do it. I told Liang I had to go out and get the money. I left him with a girl, who entertained him, then fed him a dinner, and encouraged him to drink wine and gin. It took me an hour to find my men."

"One of them conked him on the head and knocked him unconscious, and then the other one shot him," said Kennelly.

"The same man who hit him also shot him," said K'ang. "The other man was just a backup, and he helped carry away the body."

"What did you pay them?"

"Pills," said K'ang. "I gave them five hundred pills apiece."

"You're gonna give us their names, of course."

K'ang shrugged.

The President ground the butt of a Camel into the ashtray in front of him on the table. The others watched him as if he were discharging some momentous historical duty. Everyone was conscious that this hour of accusation and confession had reached a point where more issues had to be resolved or they were left with nothing more significant than the condemnation of the unhappy Henry K'ang.

Mrs. Roosevelt was more conscious of this than any of the others. "I return to a basic fact," she said firmly. "You can no longer evade the evidence, Mr. Weng, that you brought an unauthorized person into the White House last Wednesday evening. I believe it is time we heard your explanation, if you have one."

"I owe no one any explanation," said Weng. "Am I on trial here?"

"The evidence is also plain that the person you brought in was Mr. George Shen, who was murdered between 5:48 when he signed in, using the name Liang P'ing, and 8:57 when his body was discovered. Mr. Shen was carrying a document written in a Japanese code. What is more, Mr. Shen understood that code, since he wrote a letter to Miss Chin Yu-lin, containing a message in that code. It is impossible to reach any other conclusion but that Mr. George Shen was a Japanese spy."

"In Anglo-American jurisprudence," said Weng, "there is a technical term I cannot recall. It means building an assumption on an assumption, one on top of another, until a wholly erroneous conclusion is reached."

"Our assumptions, Mr. Weng, are not built on assumptions," said Mrs. Roosevelt. "They are built on facts. If you wish to contest the case against you, do so on the facts."

"You are a dead man, Little Father," said Madame Chiang. "Here you are a Japanese spy, a murderer or accessory to murder; and in China you are a traitor."

"Let me hear more of your assumptions, Mrs. Roosevelt," said Weng Guo-fang.

The First Lady glanced at the stenotype operator, who had signaled that she needed to replace the fan of paper in the tray of her machine. Mrs. Roosevelt waited until the young woman nodded that she was ready.

"George Shen was not a very able man. Miss Chin Yu-lin will attest to that. He had made his living as an interpreter, English-Chinese-Japanese. When war came, he lost his position. For some odd reason, he did not find another, although one would assume his talents would have been in demand. He was forced to live in reduced circumstances, and he was bitter. He had visited Japan and probably made contacts. Maybe he had already committed himself to a Japanese intelligence service before the war came. Maybe he had been handing over secret information about shipping and so on, for some years. In any event—"

"He'd do anything for a buck," Chin Yu-lin interjected. "I ain't even *told* you what he'd do. He figured he was entitled. He—"

Mrs. Roosevelt turned toward the girl. "I want to ask you something, Miss Chin," she said. "How many letters did you ever receive from George Shen?"

"Just the one. Just the one you found in my room."

"Could you swear he wrote it? Did you ever see any other samples of his handwriting?"

Chin Yu-lin shook her head.

"Let me tell you what I assume, Mr. Weng," said Mrs. Roosevelt. "Let us do talk about building assumption on assumption. Let us talk about impossible coincidences."

"Amuse yourself," said Weng Guo-fang.

"Some Japanese intelligence officer," she said, "decided to make a little gambit. He decided it would be useful somehow to make the United States believe a Japanese naval task force was about to enter the Indian Ocean and the Bay of Bengal. How in the world could he make the United States believe that? How better than to deliver to the United States government a dead spy—one with a coded document on him, written in a code the Japanese knew, or suspected, the United States had broken."

Weng Guo-fang shook his head and grimaced scornfully.

"How to make that spy look important?" she went on. "How better than to get him into the White House? And what an opportunity presented itself! Three Japanese agents—yourself, Mr. T'sa Yuang-hung, and Mr. Liang P'ing—would be spending two weeks in the White House in February."

"Amuse yourself . . ."

"I imagine you did not like your orders, Mr. Weng. You are too clever to imagine the plot would succeed. In the first place, why should the spy *die* in the White House? Why should he be *murdered* here? If one of our guards had killed him . . . But, of course, there was no way to work that out. Your orders were to bring into the White House a not-very-bright and expendable agent—and kill him here. I suppose Mr. T'sa Yuang-hung and Mr. Liang P'ing killed him. Who else? You would have liked to kill Mr. Shen in the

Situation Room on the ground floor, but that was too well guarded. So you led him into the Map Room on the second floor: a poor second choice."

"Bravo . . ." said the President quietly.

"Even poor George Shen had better sense than to carry an important coded message in his pocket while carrying out what he had to know was a risky mission. So there is no Ben, of course. And Mr. Shen was not carrying the message. It was put in his pocket after he was dead. Mr. Shen did not write the letter Miss Chin was carrying—which she had innocently accepted as a love letter. It was written by one of you.

"There are other details," Mrs. Roosevelt went on. "You, Mr. Weng, came to the White House in advance of Madame Chiang. You established a pattern of going in and out, so the gate guards would come to know you and your comings and goings would attract no notice. Mr. Liang never went out, so the guards would not know him. But of course they had his name in their book, as one of Madame

Chiang's party, and you had no difficulty in passing Mr. Shen through as Mr. Liang."

"What about the pills?" asked Madame Chiang. "What did they have to do with everything?"

"They were to deliver them to Mr. K'ang to help him finance Japanese espionage operations in the Washington area. Is that not so, Mr. K'ang?"

K'ang nodded. "I was told to expect we were going to get more active."

Weng Guo-fang smiled. "As you suggested, Mrs. Roosevelt," he said, "you have built assumption on assumption. I know enough of Anglo-American jurisprudence to know you cannot sustain a prosecution on the little evidence you have."

"You are probably correct, Mr. Weng," said Mrs. Roosevelt. "So I suppose we can't prosecute you. Or Mr. T'sa Yuang-hung. Instead, we will simply deport you, back to China, to Chungking."

"*No!*" yelled T'sa Yuang-hung. "Do you have any idea what they will *do* to us?"

The President was lighting another cigarette, and he paused and observed,

"I'm afraid that *is* going to be a problem for you," he said. "But what else can we do? We really have no choice."

"I'll *give* you a choice," said T'sa Yuang-hung. "I'll confess everything! Then you'll have enough evidence to prosecute us here."

The President glanced at Madame Chiang, who had stiffened with indignation. "Well . . ." he said. "Then, I suppose, we can accommodate you in an American prison."

Epilogue

Madame Chiang Kai-Shek returned to the White House in June, after a triumphal tour of the United States, and urged the President to allow Mrs. Roosevelt to accompany her back to China. The President said that visit would have to be postponed, because the First Lady was about to embark on a tour of the South Pacific.

Mrs. Roosevelt did in fact tour the South Pacific that summer, visiting not only Australia and New Zealand but even Guadalcanal. As ever, she was preceded by unkind rumors, chief among which was that she favored making every G.I. in that theater of war remain out of the United States for six months after the war ended, to be "re-civilized." The men who met her as she toured the hospitals and camps did not believe it. She was welcomed with great enthusiasm, everywhere.

The President journeyed to Cairo in

November and there at last met General
issimo Chiang Kai-shek. He realized withir
a few hours that he had already met the
dominant member of the Chiang partner
ship. He found Chiang a severely limited
provincial man, with little understanding c
the world beyond the precincts of warlore
politics.

Mrs. Roosevelt's invitation to visi
China was again pressed and again de
ferred.

She did not, in fact, ever visit China
Madame Chiang returned to the State.
from time to time. She lived on, into the
1990s, sustaining her myth and much c
her influence to the end.

Agent Robert Kirkwal was woundec
defending President Truman against an at
tack by Puerto Rican gunmen. After tha
he retired from the Secret Service and
wrote a book about his White Hous
years.

Weng Guo-fang and T'sa Yuang-hung
were tried before a United States Distric
Court in secret session and sentenced to
life imprisonment. Henry K'ang was al
lowed to plead guilty to treason. All other
charges against him were dropped in re

urn for his cooperation. He, too, was sen-
enced to life in prison.

The men who killed Liang P'ing were
ried for murder, sentenced to death, and
he sentence was carried out, by hanging,
n July 1943.

The three Chinese—Japanese—

Weng Guo-fang, seventy years old,
entered the prison hospital immediately on
his arrival at Alcatraz and never occupied
a cell there. He was moved within a week
o a federal hospital facility, where he died
n August.

T'sa Yuang-hung was imprisoned at
Alcatraz until November 1949, when he
was transferred to the Southern California
Metropolitan Correction Center. He remained there until June 1960, at which
ime he was granted a parole conditioned
on deportation to China. His wife, whom
he had not seen since 1941, had become
a district leader of the Chinese Communist
Party. She had asked for him through the
nternational Red Cross. He returned to
China and was committed by his wife to
a political re-education center, where he

remained for fourteen months. After tha
he became a teacher of American Englisr
in Peking.

Henry K'ang, too, was transferred from
Alcatraz in 1949. He was moved to the fed
eral penitentiary in Atlanta. He was parolec
in 1968, having served twenty-five years o
his sentence for treason.

Fuzzy Cairns served fifteen years fo
selling the pills that killed Barbara Lowe.

Chin Yu-lin went home to San Fran
cisco. She loyally kept the secrets she hac
learned in Washington, and was sponsorec
by Mrs. Roosevelt for a scholarship tc
Stanford University. She was not a suc
cessful student and left the university afte
one semester. Annoyed by her failure, she
enrolled herself in a series of correspon
dence and night courses and in 1945 ap
plied for admission to UCLA. She wa:
accepted, graduated in 1950, and became
a teacher in the Los Angeles public
schools. She married a police officer and
became the mother of five children.

Japan lost the war. So did China.